THE
BETRAYAL

A RED CELL NOVEL

THE BETRAYAL

John Kalkowski

THE BETRAYAL
A RED CELL NOVEL

iUniverse books may be ordered through booksellers or by contacting:

iUniverse
1663 Liberty Drive
Bloomington, IN 47403
www.iuniverse.com
1-800-Authors (1-800-288-4677)

Because of the dynamic nature of the Internet, any web addresses or links contained in this book may have changed since publication and may no longer be valid. The views expressed in this work are solely those of the author and do not necessarily reflect the views of the publisher, and the publisher hereby disclaims any responsibility for them.

ISBN: 978-1-4917-7369-7 (sc)
ISBN: 978-1-4917-7371-0 (hc)
ISBN: 978-1-4917-7370-3 (e)

Library of Congress Control Number: 2015914731

Print information available on the last page.

iUniverse rev. date: 10/20/2015

For Max and Lucy—
two future red teamers.

August 6, Baghdad, Iraq
Azad

He had never before been repulsed by death. His usual intrigue had decayed at the sight of his best friend being lead to the gallows. The noose collared about Umar Ghazi's neck seemed almost impatient with its downward tug. It was thicker than Azad expected. The weighted burden visibly pulled at Umar's spine and forced his head to lean forward. The coarse rope appeared to embrace its duty by constricting the thin cloth wrapped beneath Umar's bearded face. Looping through an iron beam clamp above him, the slack of rope dangled from the ceiling, swaying against his face with the free frolic of horrific playfulness.

A strobe effect of continuous bright camera flashes haunted the dimly lit balcony. The stains of soul-thirsty apparitions appeared to leak from peels in the ceiling's plaster. As the flashes sprung through each metal railing, Azad swore he could see other shadowy horrors reaching out expectantly for his friend. This was a ghastly place to die.

Averting his eyes to the balcony's frame, he could see the square seams of a hinged executioner's door at Umar's shoe-tip. Light streamed through the cut-away slits that edged the wooden false-floor into the dizzying emptiness between them.

He pulled away from the corner where he had been standing, mixing into the crowd of witnesses. He wanted a closer look above at the bound man he had once called "Brother." It did not matter if he was seen—no one else here would know of the two years he had spent holed-up in a secret training facility working closely with the younger man to learn the tactics

1

of cyber espionage. Using his skills to obtain falsified security hadn't been that big of a challenge and was worth the risk; he owed this much to Umar.

As if in a defiant statement of purity, he decided, Umar was dressed in an all-white two-piece thobe with simple buttons down the front and a pocket on the left chest side. The square-cut tail of his shirt hung to his knees and covered most of his white cotton pants. For the bindings at his wrists, his sleeves had been slightly rolled to his forearms. Smartly dressed, Umar could have passed as a common businessman on any marketplace corner instead of the hate-filled terrorist that he had become.

He watched as a guard cloaked in a black mask urged Umar forward onto the platform with a pull of his arms. Dragging his leg forward with a limp, Umar unsteadily stepped onto the floorboards as sagging creaks uttered their anticipation. Raising a free hand, the guard offered him a blackened hood.

"Do not cover me!" the condemned man spat and shook his head violently sideways. "What? Are you trying to be humane? This," Umar continued, thrusting his chin toward the noose hanging loosely around his neck, "is no more humane than what America has done to any of us. And you want to hang me for fighting back? For trying to rid our lives of the humiliation and disgrace they have caused us? Their greed has led brother to fight against brother! And you are condemning me for trying to end all of it? Am *I* not the humane one?"

Nodding his head in agreement, he liked how his friend continued to fight. Pulling his cell phone from his jeans pocket, he hit the video icon with his thumb. He swung his arm around to pan the crowd; there were others that would want to see this and perhaps even use it to promote their cause. To ensure his friend's legacy, he would upload this final plea to the internet. Looking at the eager crowd, his own anger rose as he decided to make the disposal of each person identified from this video Umar's eulogy.

"The Americans...they have turned me over to you—my own country—as a symbol of trust," Umar continued.

He felt Umar's unblinking stare tear through the silence of the room, as it demanded attention, those hate-filled eyes intent upon persuasion. "They expect justice for my actions in Chicago last year. You are my witnesses that

I have done nothing wrong. The Americans are the murderers of innocent lives. The only true justice is for them to experience the very same. America killed millions of blameless civilians in Hiroshima; it wasn't considered a *crime* of war. They called it justified! How is that any different than my part in attacks against them? With what they have done to the rest of the world, were my actions not also justified?"

The hooded guard seemed unaffected by the comments as he pulled the hardened slipknot to the doomed terrorist's shoulder in preparation for the drop. Umar's gaze automatically dropped to the flat timber below his feet. The boards sagged; a lip of edged wood revealed the trip door bowing beneath his body. Its hinges held firm, not yet ready to give in.

An unwavering voice from the guard boomed through the silence, "FIVE!"

"American foreign policy deserves retaliation!"

"FOUR."

"Think of all the violence, assassinations, overthrown governments," he stammered as if trying to appeal to any faltering sympathies. And with begging tipped at the rise of his eyebrows, "Torture tactics?"

"THREE...TWO."

"You can't do this to me!" he pleaded through short-breathed screams.

And, as Umar looked downward, their stares connected.

He saw the recognition flash in Umar's eyes and then noted the considerable fear clenched at Umar's teeth as a streak of sweat dripped from the man's brow.

"ONE."

Wild-eyed, the man about to be hanged tensed.

He saw Umar's knees bend as if he was preparing to leap. The grating sound of the lever and the creak of the hinges below the bound feet began to whine in unison. Umar's body visibly shuddered as his back straightened with rigidness.

Unhinged, the door sagged. Giving way to Umar's weight, the spreading wooden planks fell open past their stationary frame. The folded slack of rope began to pull apart with tension.

A sudden empathetic catch of air seized at the back of his own mouth as he watched the drop.

Before Umar's final breath could dissipate through unresponsive lips, the man made his last rancorous petition to the world. Instead of pleading mercy, his friend wailed out for desperate vengeance against the one responsible for his imminent death. The perpetual fury of the condemned man's voice echoed throughout the room, battering its palpable heat into every eardrum. The haunting tone, a shrieking bawl, stretched out with an undying last consonant sound, "WILL CONLANNNN!"

October 16, Mount Prospect, Illinois

8:30 A.M.

"Your mom's going to kill you!" Ryan blurted over his best friend's shoulder through a half-choked laugh. The online grade portal on Will Conlan's computer screen illuminated the "F" that had been reported for his English grade. Ryan's shock broke the silence of the normally quiet media center that doubled as a study hall room during first period.

Not realizing the underlying amusement buried in his friend's words, Will sat unblinking through the hue of the backlit screen. "This *can't* be right. I just submitted that English paper yesterday. I know I had an 'A' before then."

"Mr. Snodgrass must hate you even more than Mr. Tenepior seemed to last year."

Will knew his best friend was referring to their previous English teacher who had focused an overwhelming stream of negative attention toward Will before being forced to disclose his actual identity. Mark Tenepior, a chief CIA operative, had gone undercover as a teacher last year to covertly begin utilizing Will's unhindered imagination to help outthink a deceptive terrorist threat. The operation had succeeded in dissolving the destructive cell and subsequently led to the mysterious retirement of their former teacher.

"I couldn't have screwed up the paper *that* bad."

"Not saying you did—you just seem to have bad luck with English teachers," stated Ryan.

"Yeah, but at least Mr. Tenepior managed to save my life a couple of times. This guy might just make me lose it," retorted Will, considering the probable parental punishment awaiting him at home.

"Not if it's actually a mistake. Why don't you try refreshing your screen to see if it was just a glitch?" encouraged Ryan.

Pushing his mouse forward, Will pressed the circular blue arrow icon. A second later the spooling page regenerated the data on a fresh screen. Charted next to the English course listing remained the "F." Below it registered another "F" for his AP history course. In fact, every class charted in the spreadsheet now displayed a failing grade.

Stunned, Will tried shaking mysterious cobwebs from his brain to rattle loose the impossibility of what had just happened. Moments earlier the only grade that didn't average to an "A" was English. In place of the normal 4.0 was a calculated decimal, that despite being smaller in score, filled the screen with its obscenity. Each "F" punctuated the page like a vertical row of explanation points.

Mouth agape, Will asked, "What in the world? Ryan, are you seeing what I am seeing?"

"Holy cow. Didn't you just have a bunch of 'A's' before that? Refreshing usually fixes broken webpages for me," Ryan replied as if he thought this might help out.

"When have you seen me ever flunk anything?" Will retorted. "Look at these. All 'F's'? Something's going on."

"Yeah. That computer's messed up. Remind me never to click on that refresh button again."

"This is serious, Moritz! These are my grades."

"Maybe it's a reality check, man. The great Will Conlan comes back down to earth to join us normal people. Perhaps the grades are real? Could your mind be too stuck on a certain Miss Stacey again?" Instantly, Will's arm jerked backward to elbow Ryan. "Hey, I'm just saying it's happened before," Ryan interjected and pulled his arms in front of him as a playful attempt to ward off Will's next likely blow.

"There's no *too* much thinking about that," Will replied with a curt shake of his head as he twisted halfway around in his chair to face Ryan.

Not only was Stacey Chloupek beautiful, quick-witted, and as gifted an athlete as any in their high school, Will was insanely crazy about her and easily distracted in her presence. "But in all honesty, I can see one teacher making an error on a grade, but all of them?" Waving a backhand at the monitor, he spoke, "Something fishy's going on. It's gotta be a computer glitch. This is just messed up."

Still trying to make light of the unusual situation, Ryan asked, "You sure you aren't somehow logged into Kyle's grades instead of yours?"

Managing a small grin, Will stated, "Would have normally thought so myself, but that's my name listed in the heading," emphasizing his point by jabbing his index finger toward the page's name field.

"Hey, you guys talking 'bout me?" snorted Kyle from a row of desks over to the right. Though they were all friends, Kyle had a way of pressing everyone's buttons when he felt like being obnoxious. Being a captain on the freshman football team had earned Kyle the clout to hold his head in a cocky air of superiority and loose his ungrounded comments with a free pass.

"Great," muttered Will, not anxious to have Kyle know anything of the situation involving his grades.

But before Will could exit out of the grade report, Kyle appeared behind him, obviously wanting to be included in the conversation. "Oh, man! What happened to you? You're flunking every class?" The surprise forced his voice to raise an extra decibel in volume, alerting all their fellow students in study hall to Will's predicament and starting a chorus of murmuring throughout the room.

He turned back to face the screen and spat, "Thanks Kyle. Now everybody knows."

"You should probably talk to Mr. Snodgrass in 5th hour about your English grade before your mom finds out," offered Ryan.

"Yeah, you're right. I'll talk to him. He'll be able to figure out what's wrong with the grade program. I know it wasn't the paper I wrote. The writing may not have been perfect, but I'm sure my ideas were solid."

Kyle pressed his nail beneath a specific line on the screen. "You flunked P.E.?" Spitting out a chuckle, he joked, "How does a person flunk P.E.? Doesn't sound real solid to me."

"Or maybe he got my paper mixed up with someone else's?" Will offered the possibility, as if trying to pin the fault on Kyle.

Quite openly, Kyle stated, "Couldn't have been mine. 'Snotgrass' doesn't have it, yet. Was going to turn it in today, but now I think I'll wait to see how much he yells at you first."

11:14 A.M.

Will entered his English classroom with over a minute left in passing period. He walked around a row of desks and steered himself directly toward Mr. Snodgrass so he could ask him about his grade. Will had already repeated this approach with three previous teachers. Each time, the teachers sided with Will, but couldn't seem to explain why the grade program was not matching the grade he claimed he had in each course. He hoped he'd have more success in English.

With a white-covered writing textbook under one arm, he approached the wooden corner of the teacher's desk where Mr. Snodgrass was busily pulling a textbook from his leather messenger bag.

The desk was jammed with stacks of papers and various books stacked around a laptop's docking station; the only order to the tabletop was a cleared spot around a glossy white coffee maker, pristine in its cleanliness, adorning one corner all by itself as would a favorite trophy in a display case.

"Ah, Will, glad you're here. Wanted to talk to you," Mr. Snodgrass prodded with a beckoning wave of his arm. Before Will could consent his agreement, Mr. Snodgrass continued, "I came to school early this morning anxious to score the rest of these reports, yours included in the few I didn't get finished last night. It didn't take me long to identify an area of concern with your particular choice of words." As he spoke, his fingers were pressing keys on his laptop to open a folder so he could display for Will the electronic copy saved in his digital dropbox. Paging down to the second page, Mr. Snodgrass rotated his laptop on his legs and rolled his chair closer to Will before lifting it up and handing it to him so he could read the screen.

Will bent his head toward the computer as he took it into his hands and glazed his eyes over the words Mr. Snodgrass had pointed out. *But the war is not over—and it will not be over until either we or the extremists emerge victorious.*

"Will, those are not your words. They were President George W. Bush's. One of his most famous speeches and probably my favorite all-time public address, these words came from a tribute he gave in memory of 9/11," informed Mr. Snodgrass. "You plagiarized his speech—an absolute inexcusable act. Cheating is unacceptable!" Just as these words were spoken, the bell rang, making Will feel like he had just entered a boxing match and got thrown against the ropes with nowhere to hide.

"These weren't the only lines from that speech you copied either. In fact, much of the entire paper is riddled with the words of our former President," Mr. Snodgrass continued.

"But I didn't write that in my paper!" exclaimed Will.

"Is this not your paper?" asked Mr. Snodgrass as he scrolled up to the title page noting Will's name as the author and further pointing out with his finger the paper's title at the top of the menu bar also displaying Will's name.

"Well, it *is*, but it isn't," Will tried to explain, but was quickly cut off.

"Will, I know plagiarism when I see it. Heck, turnitin.com earmarked it immediately."

"But I didn't use his words in my paper," Will interposed. With complete dismay, he couldn't figure out where any of these words had come from. These were not the paragraphs he had crafted. There was no explanation for their appearance. He had never even read any of the former President's speeches. Here he had come to challenge his incorrect grade and now he was being confronted with words he had not written.

With sarcasm practically drooling from his lips, Mr. Snodgrass continued, "Are you actually suggesting that this paper which was submitted electronically from your personal digital username actually is not the paper *you* really sent to me? Is there another Will Conlan I teach?"

"What I am saying is that the paper I sent you had only my own words in it. I don't know how those phrases got into my paper. I've never copied in my life. I wouldn't have to copy anyone else's words—I'm usually able to come up with pretty good ideas to talk about on my own. I'm a good student. You can ask any teacher."

Will stopped as he realized his error. Unwittingly, he had mentioned his supposed academic skills as his proof that he hadn't committed the heinous act on the very morning his grades somehow didn't and wouldn't back up his story.

Lifting a coffee mug from his cluttered desk and slowly taking a sip before lowering it back down to rest on a stack of papers, Mr. Snodgrass's eyes never left Will. "I've taken a look at your grades this morning, and I don't think your personal assessment of your own abilities is on par with your overall performance."

"But…but I didn't do anything wrong!" Will pleaded. Exasperated, he stammered an incoherent mumbling of "But…" and "aha…" but couldn't manage a complete retort.

Snodgrass once again paused to sip from his coffee and leaned back in his chair, cupping his mug between both hands and pursing his lips before continuing on. "I've heard you're a fine baseball shortstop. Did you know that I've done some umpiring myself?" He reached forward to place his mug onto the circular disk of the coffee maker and leaned toward Will, resting one elbow on the papers of his desk.

"I'd like to use an anecdote from my officiating days to help you understand this situation in terms you may better identify with. Sometimes an 'out' on a close play is based on which player was being a bonehead. If a dumb move made the play close, an umpire may call an 'O.B.S.' because the player deserved an 'Out for Being Stupid.' I believe this paper of yours definitely qualifies as an 'O.B.S.'"

"I understand what you are telling me, Mr. Snodgrass. But I didn't copy any of those words into my report. They weren't in it when I sent it to you," Will implored. Here he stood knowing that he had once fought a handful of crazed terrorists and won by using his head, but now was getting raked over the coals because his jumbled mind kept putting two and two together and coming up with five. There simply wasn't a logical reason for any of this.

He was so wrapped up in their conference and so utterly confused by all this that he hadn't noticed until now that the class was all seated and listening intently to their conversation. It was as if they all had subliminally agreed to refrain from any disruptive behavior so that they could witness something way more entertaining and probably more educational than any curricular lecture could deliver. Not even a snap of bubble gum was present in that classroom.

"Why don't you then log into your server space on my laptop and show me the copy you sent so we can settle this once and for all," suggested Mr. Snodgrass with an even voice like that of an attorney who knows the answer before asking the question.

Will, anxious for vindication, was already typing in his username as his teacher finished speaking. As the file came up, Will felt relieved that he was finally going to have some concrete proof of his innocence. He couldn't believe that any of this was happening. First it was his grades changing before his eyes and then his paper had transformed into those foreign words.

But what he saw when it opened didn't seem real. The draft on his server space was identical to the copy in Mr. Snodgrass's dropbox.

11:30 A.M.

"O.K., Will. Don't panic," ordered Mr. Snodgrass. "Though I think you deserve being called out, I am not ready to throw the book at you and have you expelled for violations of academic integrity. I usually don't fall for acting skills when making calls, but I must say that you look genuinely surprised about your paper. It's quite a convincing performance. But the evidence is right there and I can't ignore it. I am willing, though, to give you another opportunity to resolve this mistake." He seemed to announce this loud enough for the rest of the class to clearly hear, making an example of Will in front of them all. "I want to believe you, though the documentation against it is overwhelming. Let me be clear that your grade will stand at the current 'F' until what I am proposing gets completed," Mr. Snodgrass offered.

Will felt that there was only one option left for him now. Without a reasonable explanation as to what was going on, an explanation that he knew existed from his hours red teaming alongside some of the brightest, most original thinkers in the country, he lowered his head to accept the proposal without contradiction.

"Despite what you claim, it seems to me that you have a problem coming up with your own original thoughts." These last words were spoken separately and deliberately with a pause between each. It took most of Will's control not to lash back, as these words couldn't be further from the truth, but he knew that if his skills weren't classified as a matter of the nation's security, this man would have known better.

"The only thing that comes to mind that may cure this is to have you write a different type of essay—an I-Search paper to be exact." The smug grin stretching across his face showed how clever he thought his own idea. "To write an I-Search, you pick a topic that you can personally connect to, and write about it from your own point of view. It's more of a personal research paper—one that has immediate relevance to your life—a topic which you truly want to know more about. Since only short specific facts will come from possible research and the rest from your own thoughts, it will be unlikely that you'll be able to plagiarize this time. Let me know what you've picked for your topic by Monday. Then you'll have until the end of the week to finish."

Finally swiveling his head back to the rest of his students who had sat in rigid silence to this point, Mr. Snodgrass rose from his seat and fixed his stare on his captivated crowd. For a moment the class just sat there, a frozen collection of quiet compliance. Resting a hand on his hip, Mr. Snodgrass slowly raised his coffee cup to his lips and swallowed once. His eyes didn't blink. With an urgent busyness, textbooks slammed open and notebooks were tugged from desk trays as the students quickly averted their eyes away from his gaze.

Leaning closer to Will's downcast head, Mr. Snodgrass whispered his next statement so that it would remain between just the two of them, "And let me remind you that if you don't comply with this written paper, I'll be forced to submit a referral for a recommended suspension."

Nodding his head just once, Will handed back the laptop and picked his textbook up from the desk corner. He turned back to his row, allowing the book in his dangling arm to bump loosely against his thigh as he shuffled to his seat. Just as he slumped into the plastic chair, the class rose to Mr. Snodgrass's direction for lunch. It would have been welcome relief for Will had it not been a split period where he'd be forced to come back to English after lunch for the conclusion of class.

As they made their way to the cafeteria, Ryan caught up to Will. "Did you really copy Bush's speech?" He smoothed over the part in his dark black hair as he spoke.

"What do you think? Of course not," Will emphatically replied.

"Reminds me of last year when you had to write that paper for Agent Tenepior. You don't think Snodgrass is with the Red Cell too?" Besides Will's parents, Ryan and Stacey were the only two people outside the CIA's employment to know of his secret government affiliation a year ago.

Will rolled his eyes. "You've got to be kidding."

"Yeah, you're right; Mr. Snodgrass would know better," concluded Ryan. As he spoke, they lined their trays up on the sliding metal track that ran along the various entrée choices in the food line. After dropping a pepperoni slice onto his tray, Ryan began tapping the counter with a pair of salad tongs as he scanned the selection of vegetables. It was obvious he was searching for something lighthearted to say. "Well, at least maybe now you'll believe me that you mix about as well with English teachers as the spaghetti, chili Fritos, and vanilla pudding you just placed on your tray."

Completely distracted in his own thoughts, Will hadn't even realized his food selection as he plunked his tray down in front of the cashier and handed her his student ID. The lunch lady swiped his card, looking blankly at the register's monitor. She turned the card over, murmured a "Humph," and swiped it again, clicking her fingernails on the stand in a rhythmic impatience. Turning to the side where her hand rested on her hip, she flatly stated through a chomp of her gum, "Sorry, Hon. Card says there's no money in your account. You'll have to put it back. We don't take negative balances."

Will shook his head. Placing his hands on top of his head, he bent his body at his waist and sucked in a deep breath through clenched teeth. Turning to the cashier, he stated, "This can't be! Mom always pays my account for the whole month."

Curling one cheek into a crooked frown like she'd heard it all before, she said, "Sorry. Tried it twice. No money."

"Can this day get any worse?" he halfway shouted, turning back toward Ryan.

Pushing his ID card forward to the cashier, Ryan said, "Just charge his on my account." Turning back to Will, he added with a grin, "You can buy mine tomorrow. No harm done. I'll just be sure to help myself to double servings of those ice cream shakes when you pay up."

Still zoning in on how his day kept compounding one painful event after another, Will wasn't even fazed by his buddy's jeering. "I feel like I'm in some old episode of the 'Twilight Zone' or something. None of this can be real, yet it's all happening."

"Hey, I know something that will cheer you up. Samantha and I were going to meet up for Kyle's football game tonight and then treat ourselves to some Capannari ice cream afterwards. Let's go get Stacey talked into it and we'll all go together. There's no way your day can continue going so bad with a plan like that to look forward too."

Normally Ryan would have been absolutely correct. Though the bizarre day getting worse seemed impossible, he knew nighttime always brought its darkness. He seemed more than certain this was one day he'd just rather see end.

"Do you have any relatives named Will Conlan?" he asked as he spewed a spray of aggravated spit over the man cowering below him in a fetal position on the floor. He readied the toe of his shoe for another kick to the man's gut if he didn't like the answer.

"No!" the man coughed out, laboring hard to breathe as he curled his knees into a tighter ball. His arms were pinned behind his back, bound by duct tape wound around his wrists. A syrupy line of blood clung to the corner of his mouth, and a blackened spot was already saturating his eye.

He had dragged this slumped man from his bed, half scaring him to death with the cold press of his pistol barrel against his head when he woke. The man's day-old scruff of white-speckled beard shadowing his cheeks and disheveled heaps of oily hair called attention to the mess he was in. Tiny bubbles of sweat were starting to spot his forehead and moisten his shirtless, hairy chest. He was only covered by a pair of flappy boxer shorts which seemed to make him even more vulnerable.

"I won't shoot you if you just give me answers."

The bound man looked up at the intruder through dense plumes of gas winding around him. The engine from a car idled in the garage, its exhaust escaping through a door left open into the house. Between opened curtains, squared outlines of yellow streetlamp light poured across the carpeted floor and allowed the intruder to see the billowing fumes swallowing the man's body.

He stood over the trembling man, and jabbed the gun's barrel toward him with each accusing word. "Your last name's Conlan, correct?"

"Yes. Roy Conlan," he whimpered and immediately braced himself as he had been kicked in the gut each time he had answered this very question.

"And you don't know who Will Conlan is?"

"No!" Roy screamed back with an exasperated intensity. "I've told you. I don't know him and I don't have any relatives in Chicago." He wheezed, coughing as he added, "Is it money you want?"

This time he hammered his knuckles across Roy's cheek for his simple insolence.

Internet search results had found only one listing in Chicago for the surname Conlan. He had checked every police database and phone directory, only coming up with this one possibility. The exhaust swirled into a whirlpool as he walked a full circle around Roy and pondered his next move. There hadn't been one shred of evidence in the home to disprove what the bound man had claimed, no family pictures decorated the walls nor were there any phone listings in the office rolodex. This appeared to be going nowhere and, as any man in his trade knew, dead ends couldn't become loose ends.

Pushing himself to his knees, Roy swiveled his head from the gun-wielding intruder to his garage, daring to ask, "Why is my car running?" The swells of exhaust clambered through the door, reflecting against the street lamps' illumination as it thickened, engulfing the room with its suffocating fumes. Panic grappled his voice as he whimpered, "You can have my car. Please, take it!" he commanded as though considering a much worse alternative.

"I see you've finally noticed the exhaust. With each breath you take, carbon monoxide is preventing your blood from carrying oxygen to your heart and brain. You've probably already noticed the headache, dizziness, and nausea. It shouldn't take much longer to kill you, unless you tell me about Will Conlan."

"Honestly, I don't know anything about any Will Conlan. I've already told you this," the man cried.

He decided the man must not be lying. He raised the gun above his head, regripping the firearm so the pistol's handle became a club.

"No! You don't have to do this!" the terrified man pleaded, never taking his focus from the gun.

With a downward swing, the stock crunched into the bound man's ducking forehead. His body slumped to the floor, unmoving. With no particular hurry, the intruder casually slipped through the front door, turning the knob's lock before shutting it behind him.

He strode across the street almost mechanically, as if he were counting his paces. He could have been grinding a toothpick as he sauntered, appearing to be completely lost in his own thoughts. Stepping into the shadows between the two houses facing the one he just left, he turned back to it as if expecting something.

The black shutters lining each window reminded him of the man's swollen, begging eyes. The white wicker chair on the front porch seemed just as lonely behind its railing and just as hopeless. This house with its arched veranda, shroud of tall maple trees, and rectangular hedges neatly decorating the sidewalk's path stood pristinely as if challenging him. Serene in its innocence, the home blended perfectly into the quiet, unsuspecting neighborhood. The calm sighs of the breeze that normally eased through the maple leaves were hushed by a stillness that even crickets had left for him to disturb.

It was the perfect backdrop for the type of chaos he loved to create. He knew he hadn't killed the man. This wasn't like the movies where a knock on the head would leave a man incapacitated for hours. He'd rouse within a matter of minutes and stumble to the dark garage to shut off his car. And when he did, in order to see, he'd have to flip on a light switch.

A smile drew across the intruder's face. The fun for him had always been in creating the havoc, not necessarily the killing. He wasn't particularly interested in having blood on his hands, unless, of course, he had to. It was simply much more fun to see someone do it to himself.

He knew carbon monoxide in its purest form is highly flammable, but because of the car's catalytic converter, the exhaust wouldn't be. It was merely a red herring—a sham to throw the man off course. The stinky fumes had been a perfect distraction and made it hard for anyone to smell the true weapon, the natural gas seeping from the four burners of the range he had turned on when he had first broken into the house—gas that would ignite instantly into a charring inferno with the tiniest of sparks.

And then he saw it.

He had been waiting to see just this.

Like a snapshot's negative burned into his retinas, he spotted the man's slumping body upright and silhouetted against a wall frame. His arm was reaching for the nearest light switch—a flip that would arc a tiny spark of electricity between two metal contacts before passing to a light bulb. Most people will seek the security of light on a frightening, dark night.

He knew the man would too.

He had been counting on it.

8:00 P.M.

"O.K. Squeeze tighter," Ryan emphasized as he held his iPhone between his fingers out in front of the foursome. He was trying to aim the camera to catch their pose with the football field in the background. Cradled closely together, Ryan, Samantha, Will, and Stacey wrapped their arms around each other, a small huddle pitted amongst the surrounding crowd of fans, and smiled back at the pea-sized lens.

Lots of light blue garments adorned the spectators who densely packed the center of the metal bleachers. A thinner spackling of fans spread to the outer edges. A square of uniformed band members sat below them nearer the field. Like a flock of quail, they blended together with a checkered grid of helmeted shakos, black feather plumes poking from the tops. A rattle of snare drums and thumps of a bass drum carried the fight song's cadence. On the track between them and the field danced a cheer squad, blue and white pompoms shaking high above their heads.

The setting sun tinged their faces as it splashed mixes of red and orange across the western horizon. Its rays deepened the golden sheen of Stacey's blond hair and exposed contrasting wisps of light brown tones. Will couldn't remove his eyes from the silky blend; he was still in awe of her tantalizing beauty. A slight breeze caught her hair, swishing weightless strands across her lips. She lifted a hand to run their lengths behind an ear; a few loose strands strayed against her smooth cheeks. The free waving flow of her hair through the wind and her perpetual glistening smile somehow intensified her feral charisma, making her at that moment seem wildly playful. Will was overcome with an urge to brush his cheek against hers. He yearned for those soft strands to whisk tickles across his own face. He wanted that smile to set on him.

As he stared, transfixed, she turned her head to Ryan, now holding his phone out for them all to see. Newly displayed as his personal Facebook profile picture, the small square image of their four cheering faces proudly proved his posted status, "At the football game trying to help Conlan get over his bad day."

Upon spotting the message, Stacey leaned in closer to Will, digging her shoulder against his side, whispering in a flirty tone, "So, is it working?" Seemingly to make sure it was, she additionally drew her arm through his and caressed his palm with delicate strokes of her fingertips before sliding her fingers between his.

"It's definitely turning out better than it started," Will honestly replied. Finding them impossible not to look at, he took note of how she crossed her smooth, long legs, tucking one hand between her thighs as she shifted her weight unevenly and pulled him in even tighter.

"How about we go top it off with a little ice cream? My treat," she proposed.

Though this was already part of the night's plan, he knew the mood was right for holding her hand, and a short saunter through the neighborhood with her at his side would make him feel as if everything was right in the world.

As their feet clanked down the rows of metal bleachers, Ryan's phone began to ring. Pulling it from the pocket of his cargo shorts and peering at the screen, he muttered to nobody in particular, "Hmm, unavailable number." As they rounded the corner past the field, stepping over the grass to a sidewalk, he answered, but no one replied. Ending the call by touching the screen, he rambled, "How do people get my number? Why would you call someone and not even talk back?"

"Yeah, I don't know why anyone would want to talk to you either," Will lightheartedly replied.

Ungripping her hand from Ryan's, Samantha, defending her boyfriend, swatted affably at Will. Stacey joined in the frolic, siding with Samantha by athletically nudging Will into her friend's swinging path to be sure he was struck by a couple of swipes before pulling him back to her.

The three-on-one teasing continued until they walked the bush-bordered brick path up the steps to the front porch of the white barn-shaped Capannari's ice cream parlor. After orders of double chocolate peanut butter crunch and black raspberry chip for Ryan and Will and cake batter for both of the girls, they rested themselves against the heart-shaped metal chair backs surrounding a wooden table. A line of people made their way past the glass counters beside them, eyeing the different flavors marked above on chalkboard menus.

Will noticed that an adult man, possibly in his mid-forties, seemed to take special notice of their group, occasionally turning from the counter to glance at them, his back to the choices of flavors and toppings. Though a sneer at the corner of his lips showed his teeth, he was otherwise handsome and carried his middle age well. His golden brown skin was weathered, but against graying stubble and lean-cut cheeks, he appeared distinguished. It was his eyes, though, that really set him apart. The spark emanating from his piercing pupils was calculating and suggested he was not to be crossed.

Will had caught the man's gazing eyes twice before he averted his stare and quickly turned back around. If this man was sneaking a peek at the girls, Will was going to flip. He had become increasingly aware of how boys at school seemed to rest their scanning eyes on Stacey in the hallways, but just didn't expect an older man to be doing the same.

No one else seemed to sense the creepy presence of the black-clad Peeping Tom, the girls in deep conversation about the miniature ice cream cone flower pots. Maybe it was how the man dressed that bugged Will. It was a warm fall night and yet this man wore a jacket. Or maybe it was just his stare? Will had to interrupt Ryan from his humorous imitation of the cheesy cow's grin of Capannari's mascot to nod toward the man and back to the door to suggest they leave.

Leaving small, colorful swirls puddling in the glass dishes, they rose from their seats, chair legs scuffing the wooden floor. Out of the corner of his eye as he walked toward the door, Will caught the man's head, eyes radiating a bloodshot malevolence, turn to watch them leave. Will was reminded of a similar hate-crazed gaze a year before as he was bound by rope and abducted at knife point, a cloth stuffed down his throat as a gag.

Shuffling down the steps, they walked back the way they'd come, passing middle class houses with neatly trimmed lawns. He guessed these homes were alive with Friday night parties from the many nice vehicles lining the curbs. The smell of grass and cottonwood trees flowed through the gentle breeze. As the sun set, darkness enveloped the outdoors, streetlamps illuminating small glowing spheres of yellow radiance down on the pavement. Without the hue of lights that spotlighted the streets, everything else was cloaked in darkness.

From behind them in the shadows of tall bushes and curbside cars stepped the man who had followed them out of the ice cream shop. Creeping up to no more than a dozen feet behind, he called out with a low growl, "Will Conlan?"

Instinctively knowing who it had come from, Will grabbed for both of the girls' arms to tug them forward. If disastrous things hadn't been a recurring theme to his day, Will may not have reacted as he did; he had been too on edge not to recognize trouble, especially when it was calling him by name. Ryan was the one who turned, obviously recognizing his friend's name and wanting to see who it was that called it out.

That's when the man charged, one hand out in front of him from which a pink electric arc flickered with a humming crackle. Ryan's blocking arm was met by the full contact of a drive stun. The burst of voltage coursed through his entire body as the stun gun jabbed directly into his forearm. Loud pops sizzled against his skin breaking the night's calmness.

Ryan instantly jerked back, muscles contracting as if the air had been knocked out of him, a garbled "Umph" caught at his throat. Stumbling with disorientation, his body convulsed in wild wrenching motions as the pursuer continued pressing the forked electrodes into his skin, not relinquishing his attack. Ryan, now a mere fly frying in a bug zapper, fell to the ground, limbs involuntarily flailing with uncontrollable twinges.

Samantha cried out with a horrifying shriek, "Ryan!" as her hands went to her face. Will instantly tugged Stacey backward, but she swiveled and ripped her arm free from his. Fueled by her natural athletic aggression, she rushed toward the attacker and thrust a well-aimed kick straight at his mid-section.

It was a move the man must have anticipated.

He thrust his weapon outward as her foot came near and pitched his left leg over Ryan's crumpled body like a sweeping goal kick. His shin smacked solidly into her calf, punting her leg sideways into the outstretched stun gun. Its electrical arc popped as it sank into her kneecap. She cried out.

Horrified, Will screamed an order, "Run! Samantha, get away from here!" She hesitated, looking back at the direction from which they had come, where people would be, a path that was also barricaded by the man, and ran the other way.

As he yelled, Will threw himself at the man's back, grabbing at his jacket and back pocket, anything to give him purchase enough to throw him away from Stacey and break the electricity's contact. Pulling with all his might, Will heaved backward, tugging the man away from her, the jeans pocket tearing loose in his hand. As the current broke, muscle spasms contorted Stacey's body, buckling her other leg underneath and causing her to fall, her head banging against Ryan's knee as she folded to the sidewalk into a discombobulated heap.

While being tugged, the attacker twisted and threw his arm backward, the stun gun swinging dangerously close to Will's chest. Contorting his body to avoid the current, Will dodged to one side. From the damage done to his friends, he knew he had to avoid getting stunned at all costs. This man was after him, and he didn't want to be abducted like last year.

Frantically, Will sidestepped swipe after crackling swipe with agile shuffles. Leaping over Stacey onto a lawn, his leg banged against a wire "For Sale" sign. Reaching forward, he ripped it from the sod with one hand. Knowing almost anything could become a weapon if handled correctly, he lashed back with a swing of the sign. Though only made of flimsy wire and plastic, its metal stakes slapped the man's wrist, knocking the stun gun from his grasp.

But Will failed to notice that at the very same moment his attacker had been swinging a left hook. It caught him squarely on the cheek. Falling to one knee, as unsettled as if he had been stunned, Will's focus became momentarily foggy. With a pounce, the man hurled his body on top of him, punching frantically at anything he could hit, simply overpowering Will with his strength and weight. Will tried to block with his forearms, but each blow contorted his body with painful spasms that exposed him to less impeded punishment.

Finally the man pushed his body off and kicked Will once more for good measure in the gut. His attacker moved a couple of feet away, pawing the ground for his stun gun.

Will rolled into a curl facing the street, his cheeks bulging like he might throw up, when his eyes rested on a parked BMW. With a glimmer of hope, Will's realized that any car this nice would have a built-in alarm. Triggering it might be his only salvation.

Just then, the loud pop of an electric arc crackled behind him. He had no doubt the stun gun had been found. Figuring he'd only have another second or two, he clawed the grass with his fingers for any rock. The lawns were simply too well manicured for a loose stone to be so out of place.

As blades of grass slipped through his fingers, his hand brushed against the Velcro patch that lined Ryan's shorts' pocket. Pulling out Ryan's iPhone, the only thing around that might be heavy enough to do some damage, he hurled it with all his might at the car's window. The wild throw flipped the rectangular phone end-over-end like a helicopter's rotating blades until it smacked a folded crease into the BMW's aluminum door. Blaring blasts of honks and flashing lights bellowed its distress call.

Loud and erratic, the screeching horn spooked the night's temerity. Turning his gaze, Will spied the attacker retreating into shadows. Moments later, loud yells came from a nearby porch as several people ran toward the car. In the distance he could hear Samantha's shouts as she was also making her way back with people to help, flashlights bobbing with their strides. People crouched and crowded around Stacey and Ryan to give them aid.

"Kids, are you all right?" one young man asked.

Stacey and Ryan both started coming around, each complaining of headaches and burn marks. Crawling over the ground toward Stacey, Will wrapped an arm around her neck. He pulled her toward him in an embrace, burying his face in her hair—this time from solace and not out of desire.

A police siren cried an undulating wail behind them.

His embracing Stacey along with Samantha's brief story seemed to confirm the crowd's suspicions and little fuss was given over the dented car. That had not been vandalism. Their caring hands immediately attended the kids' needs and back pats of praise were given to Will for his quick thinking.

Sighing with relief now they were out of danger, Will rose from his knees, trying to balance himself against the ground with a hand. Only then did he notice, still firmly gripped in his left hand, the square of blue corduroy that had been his attacker's pocket. Loosening his grip, the pocket unfolded. Crumpled within the crevice, a twice-folded sheet of computer paper slipped out. Lifting one corner of the folded paper and bending it back, Will saw an image that startled him more than anything that had happened that day. Gasping, his breath caught in his throat. What he saw simply seemed unreal. Like a dangerous secret meant not to be shared, he immediately shoved the crumpled square into his pocket.

With his one look, he now knew for sure that this attack had been premeditated. But for one to carry it out this quickly meant something Will was not prepared to handle. On the printed page Will had seen a reflection of himself, arm-and-arm with three of his closest friends attending a ballgame that had only ended forty minutes before.

10:10 P.M.

Will opened the door of the police car and stepped out onto the walkway leading to his house. His parents met him at the door. After a brief explanation from the officer detailing the cunning Will had displayed to foil a mugging, his parents allowed their shoulders to sag, relief replacing the concern flowing from their previously uptight bodies. Pulling back at an arm's length and really taking a look at Will, his mother said, "Your cheek and arms are all bruised."

"My side is too," Will winced, appreciating the attention.

"But, if it wasn't for your son's quick thinking," the officer quickly added, "it could have been a lot worse."

Shutting the front door after thanking the policeman, they hugged Will tight, his dad rapping him on the shoulders with pride. His mother said with wonderment, "We don't know how you continue to get mixed up in these things, but we are glad you and your friends are O.K."

His father had a different way of expressing his relief. With good humor, his father kidded, "Maybe we should hire a bodyguard for him—probably be cheaper than auto repair." And in his fatherly way, he masked his obviously shaken nerves as he joked, "Did you really have to pick on a BMW? Couldn't have opted for an old Studebaker? That's going to cost us a fortune."

His dad's good nature made it hard for him to allow the mugging lie to pass, but he hadn't really had a chance to sort out in his mind all that had occurred. The day had been one disaster after another. He still didn't know what to think about the folded picture or that he had been intentionally tracked down. He knew it was best to be honest with his parents, but after his involvement in top secret CIA operations, Will had become very good at hiding the truth. Until more of this made sense, he thought it best to keep his parents in the dark. If they knew the real danger, they'd never let him out of their sight. The last time someone had personally attacked him, he had almost been strangled to death.

Now it was his mother's turn to counter with something she *did* know. "It seems as if trouble has been following you around today."

The statement caught Will off-guard. He'd almost forgotten about the horrid disaster his report had become with everything else the day had included. He hadn't anticipated having to defend himself in the safety of his own home.

Will's pause gave his father chance to prod, "Anything else you'd like to tell us about? You know, lettin' the cat outta the bag is a whole lot easier than puttin' it back in."

Normally the phrase would have made Will chuckle, but he sensed their firmness; both statements had been free of accusation and open enough to give Will an opportunity to come clean. Will carefully phrased his reply, "Mr. Snodgrass basically asked me to rewrite my paper." He was trying to avoid the punishment that would come if they believed he had actually cheated and there was no way he could explain how those copied words ended up in his paper anyway. Reluctant to say more since he didn't know what his mother had found out, he waited for her reply.

"I happened to run into Mr. Snodgrass at the game tonight and he told me much the same. He wasn't real forthright about why you have to write the report, but assured me that your grade would improve once it is completed. In any case, don't you suppose there's still a little time tonight to get started on it before bed?" It was her gentle way of explaining a requirement.

He weighed the possibility of arguing against homework on a Friday night or pointing out that it'd be hard to concentrate after the attack, but knew arguing might cause his parents to inquire more about the paper. And besides, it was an argument he was sure to lose. Will understood his parents had always been sticklers about homework, on week nights, requiring its completion before anything else. Begrudgingly, he pulled a spiral notebook out of a kitchen drawer and shuffled off to the dining table to begin his draft.

As he predicted, Will found it impossible to concentrate with so many things about the day's events swirling around his mind. He couldn't shake the frustration of how things had spiraled out of his control. Grades he knew were "A's," a lunch account that was always paid in full, and a paper that he knew to be submitted correctly all puzzled him. What pressed him even more was the fact that most of his Saturday would be secretly spent red teaming, role playing scenarios in search of tactical clues that would enhance America's defense strategies with a bunch of creative experts who had come to expect answers of Will for the inexplicable. How could he possibly offer any real insight into the protection of an entire country when he wasn't able to figure out even little things in his own life?

The question nagged at him, anxiety tugging at his stomach for the logical world to resurface, people walking upright and trees rooted to the ground. Because of his youth, he had always felt an extra pressure to prove himself and being at a loss for answers burdened that feeling even more.

There was really only one place in his life where he felt like the answers came more naturally to him. His gift to see into hidden possibilities had helped foil two large-scale terrorist attacks. It had earned him a role sharing ideas with the nation's intelligence leaders. Maybe he'd gotten lucky. Or maybe he really was able to think beyond the boundaries of reason that held back most people from opening their minds. He'd show Mr. Snodgrass just how original his thoughts really were. His involvement with the CIA helped define who he believed he was and what he was destined to do.

So that's exactly what Will started writing about. Mr. Snodgrass had said that an I-Search paper was one that he had a need or a genuine desire to know more about. If he were to have a beneficial role in stopping future terrorist plots against the U.S., he'd definitely need to know more on how terrorists would go about such attacks. And it just so happened that he was to meet with a Red Cell tomorrow to brainstorm such a scenario. Satisfied that the topic was somehow meant for him, he titled his page, "How to Pull off the Perfect Act of Terrorism."

He then started with a personal story, one which had him in study hall at school a year ago, turning on the TV to see the billowing clouds of dust and scattered shards of black glass surrounding the Sears Tower after an explosive-packed bus detonated that fall morning. Discussing what it felt like for his home turf of Chicago to be attacked, he described his impression of being so closely connected to the event. After describing the pride and enthusiasm of being a part of the home crowd at Wrigley

Field for the Cubs' first resumed game just two days after the attack, he established the reasons for his interest in this I-Search topic.

He then continued laying out the parameters. He wrote, "A small scale attack would have a greater chance at success. Large-scale coordinated attacks," he reasoned, "require too much planning and too many resources to implement without arousing suspicion." He did admit, though, the fundamentals of the plot he'd worked out could be applied to a catastrophic event if the target lacked substantial security measures. He chose to plan his make-believe attack to take place in a crowded public area. He explained that the ideal would be to strike frequently to arouse fear and overwhelm a shaky economy. For this report, though, he would limit his plan to a one-time event to minimize the pre-operational steps it would take to enact.

The difficulty, Will realized, with choosing this topic was that he wouldn't need to research information; in fact, he might even have to fudge his wording to prevent divulging top secret information. He didn't need any quotes from statisticians to support his ideas; the Red Cell had immersed him in hundreds of pages of classified documents on counterterrorism over the past year. The information wouldn't need to be extracted from some secondary expert who had spent his life in a college classroom studying terrorism; his information was so authentic it came directly from the sources themselves, from the undercover spies entrenched deep within spotty organizations to those who advised the President of the United States on a daily basis.

Because of all this first-hand experience, coming up with his overall scheme for the paper was very simple. The plot had actually come to him months ago after reading an archived Red Cell Report on attacks that target people. After Red Cell brainstorming sessions, agents write these papers to prepare defenses for potential terrorist plots. Within this specific report, cyanide-laced Tylenol capsules were mentioned.

This gave him the perfect idea for his paper. People had to eat. In fact, each day offered the opportunity to attack the public at least three different times. If there was a way to poison the food they bought, it could create unspeakable damage. Not only did this plan kill people, but it would cause massive panic. The public would become skeptical of any food item for sale, fearful of each bite they took.

The idea was not a new one. He knew similar plots had been considered before, but each time flaws in its implementation made it an unlikely threat. There were obvious logistical problems getting the poison into the foods. Not only did dietary products have to pass routine quality and safety tests but any tainted goods would be subject to recalls effectively removing the product from the supply chain before many people were affected.

While most analysts would decide it too difficult for terrorists to manage such an attack, Will saw ways around these issues. He felt the most likely scenario would involve poisoning the food once it was already cooked. In this case, a possible taste test would be this food's only quality control obstacle. If a mobile food stand were to season its menu items with a toxin, he reasoned, it could cause several hundred deaths in a single event and its perpetrators could probably flee the scene before any suspicions are aroused. To increase casualties, multiple simultaneous attacks could take place at public events all around the country.

Will noted in his report several poisons that were not difficult to obtain that could be used to cause sufficient damage, specifically addressing those that would take many hours for the poison to take effect. The best scenario for his plan to succeed, he surmised, would be for his toxin to gradually sicken its victims. If, once exposed, symptoms wouldn't appear for hours and if the act was carried out in a public area with lots of food options, the source would be difficult to pin down and capture.

He felt it important to mention in his report some possible antidotes which he quickly checked the spellings of on the internet. The suggested cures, he countered, would be almost worthless as most people would not know they had been poisoned and thus wouldn't search out the correct cure.

Satisfied, Will trudged up to his bedroom computer. He finished for the night by typing what he had written in his spiral, now filled with more than five pages of notes and careful descriptions. The report had been frustrating to begin, but the topic itself, as he began to write, shifted his paradigm. He quickly realized how insubstantial Snodgrass's request had been, and began writing for a greater cause, one that made the effort to write it worthwhile.

Knowing his scheme might someday help the nation's security forces to divert such an attack was satisfaction enough. He felt confident that tomorrow with fellow Red Teamers, he'd have something valuable for them to discuss. What he wrote in this report could actually end up saving lives.

This sense of satisfaction pushed a wave of relaxation through the arch of his back as he stretched with a yawn. His terror plot was clever. The havoc it'd create would be devastating and hard to stop. Once in action, loads of man power and resources would be needed to counter the attack.

And these were the ideas of a teenager.

As he walked from the room, a grin curled his face as he considered that he'd truly make one heck of a terrorist.

October 17, Mount Prospect, Illinois
Azad

An eerie glow engulfed the front seat of the featureless rental car. A whitish hue from his computer screen reflected against the windshield, pushing back the surrounding blanket of darkness of the outside night. He felt the blackness press its malignant cloak through the backseat and around his shoulders. It suited the fierce scorn cutting at his heart. He had been impervious to the night's cool chilling his skin until the welcoming shudder rippled its iciness up his neck.

The clutter of crushed, plastic water bottles and crumpled fast food bags strewn across the floor mats didn't seem to bother him either. The glove compartment was open. Lodged between loose parking stubs and a black stun gun was a mobile 5G Wi-Fi Hotspot. Sprawled across the passenger's seat, a laptop leaned haphazardly against the glove compartment's door.

His eyes rapidly darted back and forth across the illuminated screen. The seal of Mount Prospect Police Department sat exposed at the webpage's corner. As one hand slid across a touch pad, the fingers on his other typed furiously across the keyboard. A smile began to form at his lips.

He raised his thick fingers to his head and excitedly brushed a smooth stroke through his dark hair. Satisfied finally, he let out a deep, lung-emptying breath. His smile stretched into a gratifying sneer as he realized what the screen was revealing. At last, on this very night, he had been gifted the opportunity to obtain authentic demographic information supplied by none other than Will Conlan himself. It had taken less than an hour and a half to crack the Mount Prospect Police Department's firewalls and access the electronic report an officer had submitted about a botched mugging earlier that evening.

The electronic incident report was meticulously detailed. Each entry blank had been completed with full accounts from each of the four teenagers involved. Displaying data even down to the zip code, the numerical address fields listed for each were going to make it all too easy to track an otherwise elusive Will Conlan right to his doorstep.

12:30 A.M.

Now feeling like sleep would come easily, Will tracked his cursor over to shut down when a password protected message window from "5663" flashed on his screen. "Good," Will said to himself, knowing that Tenepior, Will's former teacher and now his current CIA mentor, would be able to help him figure out the mess of his evening. Using top security software, Agent Tenepior had arranged for remote communication several times a week over the past year so that from home Will could continue assisting his Red Cell team to 'what if' all types of terrorist scenarios. To best protect the safety of his family and himself, this had been a secret agreement. Even his parents were unaware of their continued partnership.

Will signed in and was greeted by a typed message he hoped was sarcasm. Positioned above a blinking cursor, the words read, "If you destroy any more vehicles, Homeland Security will be forced to perform a terror evaluation on you." Will knew the agent was still irked about Will throwing a bomb under his car last year, though Tenepior had never said as much, but he still wouldn't put it past the man to request the psychological analysis to be done.

Deciding it was so rare to see Mark Tenepior, one of the most hard-core officials in the CIA, joke about something, he decided to play along and typed back, "Ha. Ha. Changing my username to 'demolition.man' tomorrow." Will liked it best when he could keep people guessing and added for good measure, "All part of my plan to terrorize the automotive industry." He knew this "fingernails-on-a-chalkboard" statement to a counter terrorism official would be the equivalent of a police officer learning someone had falsely yelled, "Fire!" in a theater.

There was dead air after his statement. Will sensed at least a couple of minutes passing without Tenepior writing back. It destroyed the satisfaction he was supposed to get from the witty comeback. Will suspected Tenepior knew this and liked using it to his advantage; after all, he was an expert at analyzing tactical situations.

At last, a question appeared on the screen. "Do you think this mugger was after something?" And like that, Agent Tenepior was all business again.

"Aren't they all?" Will continued his antics, but knew they wouldn't get him anywhere.

Tenepior, once again, didn't bite. "You and I both know this wasn't some mugging."

It never ceased to amaze Will at how unbelievably perceptive Tenepior was. How had he heard about this incident in the first place? A police scanner? Perhaps the police had shared their report with his agency? And what would a report like that contain, just facts? He knew when Agent Tenepior was his teacher he had taught his students how to draw conclusions and to make inferences, but this was bordering on the paranormal.

Will shot back, "How did you know about this anyway?"

"You have an encounter with a police officer and you don't think we'll know?"

It frustrated Will at how purposely clear and unclear his former teacher could sometimes be. He also thought it unfair that adults hated it when kids would answer a question with a question, but then they would turn around and do it themselves. But this is how it had always gone for the two of them—Tenepior would provide some insight, but only as much as he was willing to give, and Will would be forced to drop his line of questioning.

Will decided that it was Tenepior's turn to feel in the dark. "He had a print off of Ryan's Facebook page on him."

"What?" questioned, Tenepior, with such surprise that he immediately switched from messaging to their Skype-like video conferencing program usually reserved only for when Will was sure to be alone at home so they wouldn't be overheard by his parents. It was well past midnight, late enough to be of little risk because his parents would surely have been asleep in their bedroom for a couple of hours already.

"Yeah, I ripped it from his back pocket," explained Will.

The surprise hadn't rattled Tenepior for long. He quickly responded, "First a vandal and now a thief."

It was like playing chess with this guy, Will thought. When he saw an advantage, he pounced. He knew that Agent Tenepior had always acted with the seriousness inherent to his position, first as an intelligence operative with an interest in Will's youthful imagination and then as his teacher. Yet over the past year Will had seen small mellowing bits within Tenepior's joking sarcasm. The hard edge to the man was always present, but there was also a playfulness built into his wit. Will often wondered if perhaps Tenepior saw a little of his youthful self in Will which allowed him to relax and open his hardened shell when speaking to him. There was no doubt that their shared wit and endless drive to succeed bonded them. It was probably the secret to why they got along so well despite their difference in age. They had a camaraderie formed by their similar interests in provoking thought and dreaming about possibilities.

Will could see what Tenepior was up to. His kidding around usually didn't last this long and the multiple efforts to joke were an obvious effort to de-escalate Will's shock at having been attacked earlier that evening. It was just like Tenepior to try using his crisis training to control the conversation. He wanted to convince Tenepior that he was fine so he replied with the same playful tone, "That's nothing compared to the executioner I'll be dating if Stacey ever gets her hands on that guy."

Satisfied with his comeback, he decided to push on ahead with a question of his own, asking, "I get that he was able to use Ryan's Facebook status about being at a game, but how, exactly, did he find *where* we were at so quickly?"

Tenepior spoke slowly as if still thinking it through himself and trying to find the right words to explain. "The post helped him locate you, but not track you. That was most likely done by hacking into the GPS on Ryan's cell phone."

"That would probably explain the weird phone call Ryan got before we went for ice cream," Will concluded.

"Probably confirming his target," Tenepior explained. "I am guessing he created some sort of botnet or internet scan to search for any hits matching your name. It was a mistake for your buddy Ryan to tag that picture with your last name."

At all these possibilities, Will's mind reeled. With the attacker's apparent skill set, they had made themselves an easy target by naively sharing a seemingly innocent detail about themselves on the internet.

Suddenly, Will wondered about other more important details about himself out there on the web.

"You mean this guy was capable of hacking into Ryan's account?"

"Oh, that's probably not even the worst thing he could do with a cell phone. He's capable of way more than that if he was able to come across your name in the first place. Once you started working for us, for your personal safety, we made sure most of the accessible electronic data about you was hidden or removed."

"Oh, I know of at least one electronic record that still exists!" exclaimed Will.

"What are you referring to?" Tenepior wondered aloud.

"My school runs an electronic gradebook and I know for sure, now, that my grades were tampered with today. The jerk turned all my grades into 'F's'! And I just figured out what happened to my English paper. And, oh man, my lunch account!" Will rambled on with frustration until he explained the full magnitude of his day.

"I can't help you with your paper, but you won't have to worry about any other information from the grade program being shared with him. This is a precaution we took when we had all your personal information, including home address and parents' names, altered with false records. If the school would ever need to contact your parents, they'd be directed to an automated voice mail which we set up and monitor. In fact, in a moment of pure genius that I still get a laugh out of, we listed your address as the building you blew up last year across the street from our substation. Nobody will ever be able to locate your home with that info.

"No, Will, I think you are pretty safe where you are. There's not an electronic trail out there that will lead your attacker to your home." Tenepior concluded with one last remark before signing out, "I want you to get a good night's sleep. We have a big day planned at the substation tomorrow, and you just reminded me of more Red Cell Reports I need to pull for it."

CLASSIFIED
RED CELL REPORT
APPLYING ALTERNATIVE ANALYSIS TO HOMELAND SECURITY

Cyber Savagery

January 16, 2012

Summary
Handheld electronic devices pose a wide array of unique terror threat possibilities. This Red Cell team suggests that almost any technology purchased from a department store (e.g., cell phone, E-reader, garage door opener, GPS device, smartwatch, or external drive) could be modified to create a weapon. These "off-the-shelf technologies" could be used to plan attacks, share information, spread propaganda, implant viral weapons, or detonate explosives.

Nightmare Scenarios:
The Red Cell believes a carefully constructed worm or virus concealed within and deployed from a handheld or wearable technology offers the greatest potential danger. If infiltrated by a technological weapon, the following targets would be highly appealing from a terrorist standpoint because of their potential to cause massive fatalities:

- Reactor speed in nuclear power plants
- Instrument control in aviation centers
- Electrical grid systems
- Disruption to timing or routes in hubs of public transportation
- Weapons control on military bases

These are the conclusions of sixteen Department of Homeland Security Analytic Red Cell participants, a diverse group of creative thinkers and nongovernmental experts who simulated terrorist plots to brainstorm possibilities about how our country's infrastructure might be attacked. The ideas generated during this "red teaming" session are intended to help national, state, and local personnel prepare against potential casualty threats.

1:20 A.M.

From the hair dryer and cosmetics scattered around his bathroom sink, Will knew his mother would be using his hallway bathroom in the morning instead of his parents' master bathroom. She often did this when she had early weekend events to avoid waking his dad with her showering so early on a Saturday. Shoving his mom's curling iron to the side of the sink, Will pulled open a drawer and set a spool of dental floss onto the countertop. After such a crazy day and knowing he was meeting with the Red Cell tomorrow, he wanted to get his teeth brushed and be off to bed. He had already stayed up later than he'd planned to.

Days like tomorrow were the ones he most looked forward to—the opportunity to explore his imagination with the most incredible dreamers in the country: movie directors, futurists, and thriller novelists. Rooted in urgency and danger, the Red Cell's mission invigorated his life and gave it a sense of purpose. It was a world he felt he belonged to.

Running a hand through his moppy blond hair as he arched his back against a heavy yawn, Will leaned close to the mirror and gave his face a good look-over. He squeezed the skin underneath his eyes between his thumb and index finger, stretching his face against the worry lines and cheek bruise that had appeared as proof of his troubling day. Pushing his body away from the counter and rolling his head from shoulder to shoulder, he started to sleepily shuffle his feet against the tile floor to the door of the bathroom. He flicked the light switch off and took a step into the hallway toward his bedroom.

Faintly against his own quiet footsteps, Will heard a faint scratch from the floor below. It sounded like a foot sliding across the hardwood floor. This all seemed very unusual. There was no reason for one of his parents to be going anywhere at this time of night. And with his mother waking so early, it didn't seem right that she would be up now.

Then he heard the sharp choke of a car starting. He wasn't even sure the muffled sound had been a car's ignition, but such an unnatural noise was so foreign to the stillness of night, he decided it had to be. Strangely, he thought it sounded as if it had come from his own garage. His curiosity getting the better of him, he turned to go downstairs and check out the noises.

Feeling alongside the wall for the hallway light switch, he peered down the stairs directly in front of him. The instant his hand found the light, Will knew there was a problem. His hand went rigid, the switch moving upwards between his fingers. Now adjusted, his eyes spotted danger in the dark. The black cover of night was somehow too inklike. Absent in the night's dim was the glow from the Eagle Eye security panel on the wall beside the main door. The ever-present yellowish hue no longer lit up the bottom stair like a night light. There was simply blackness. The alarm wasn't just disabled; it had somehow been turned off! While his mind lingered with this realization, his fingers acted on their own accord, catching the light switch just before it flicked on and pulled it back down.

He glanced at his parent's bedroom door. For a second he considered rushing to their room. Another thought was to reach Tenepior on his computer. But he decided against both. If any tip toe creaked the hallway floor, he risked alerting this intruder.

It was easy for him to already sense what he was up against. Momentary flashes of Ryan and Stacey twitching on the ground invaded his mind. Annoyed at this particular man's persistence, a painful rage flexed at Will's arms. He couldn't help thinking this man deserved a little payback. Reveling in the fact that his home could give him the chance to inflict the punishment himself, he decided to take matters into his own hands.

Backing through the bathroom doorway, he grabbed for his mother's curling iron and gently pushed its plug into the wall jack. Squinting through the darkness, he sorted through the make-up, deodorant, and shampoo scattered about the countertop. The only other thing he found that might be of use would be his dental floss; it could be wrapped around the guy's neck to strangle him. But then he thought of a better use, if he still had time.

Lowering himself as close to the floor as he could manage, Will crawled to the edge of the stairs and wrapped one end of the dental floss around the end banister rail about a foot above the top step. He tied the line off and pulled the square plastic container across the top step. A dull grating of the plastic reel whirred as the roll of line unwound. It reverberated through the stillness of the soundless night, causing him to cringe with each murmuring rotation of the spool. Cutting through the sound of the spindle's thrumming and his own nerve, a set of three or four quick repetitive clicks ticked from the floor below. He wound the other end of his tripwire of floss around the spare bedroom's door hinge several times, the plastic container dangling from its end before he cut it loose.

As he backed deep into the bathroom, the unmistakable creak of the bottom step whined its complaint into the silence. By the slowness of it, he could tell the intruder was stepping cautiously. Will flattened against the wall, thinning himself behind the bathroom door for cover, but not before grabbing for the hot iron. It was longer and less fat than other curling irons he had seen. Opening much like the mouth of an alligator, a hinged clamp used to hold the hair in place was attached to the metal rod, now radiating heat down its entire shaft. He brandished it like a club, holding it in the air next to his shoulder, aiming to singe any piece of skin he saw.

He faced the stairs by peering through the door jamb to watch for the intruder. Wafting up the stairs with the man's movement was the faint scent of exhaust fumes. As the man came to the top of the stairs, he stepped nimbly and silently missing the trip line completely. Will caught his gasp before it left his mouth. His plan was failing before his eyes. But that's not what crushed him the most. Out in front about waist high, the intruder held a gun firmly within his grasp. He saw the weapon disappear from his crack of vision as the man pushed his way into the bathroom. Will matched his movements with the turn of his head.

The second the pistol appeared on his side of the door, Will lowered his shoulder into the back of the door like the helmet-rattling cheap shot of a defensive back cracking into a leaping receiver. Pushing off from the wall, he put all his might behind the shove. The door smashed the intruder against the Corian countertop, successfully pinning him between two hard surfaces. At the same instant, Will dropped his left hand, slapping the hot iron onto the man's thumb. The metal wand seared the heel of the palm. The clasp bit down on the top of the hand like the lockjaw of a pit bull as skin sizzled, grafting to the aluminum. The man's scream erupted through the house. He dropped the gun instantly.

Frantically the man swung his arms up and down, throwing the curling iron off and onto the floor. With a heave the intruder shoved the door back, but Will had jumped away. Swiping his hand from the corner of the countertop, Will gripped the bottle of shampoo. Squeezing the bottle's center with both hands, he let loose a stream. The syrupy liquid sprayed straight into the intruder's eyes, coating his entire face. Calling out, "Dad! Intruder!" at the top of his lungs, he imagined the shampoo digging into the man's eyes stinging and searing into bloodshot vessels.

"Da..." Will tried shouting again, but was cut off mid-word as the air from his lungs burst from impact. Charging forward in a bull rush, the intruder tackled him into the bathtub, lifting Will clear off his feet and slamming his back over the tub's edge, the shower curtain and rod crumpling on top of them.

Hardened, coarse hands grabbed for the plastic, shoving it down over Will's head as they struggled, the man's weight pinning him down. Slapping his hands around for the curtain's rod, Will seized it between his fingers and swung at the body pressing down on him. Will felt a shudder vibrate through the man's body as a cold hard slap of the aluminum rod cracked against his vertebra.

"Will?" The shouts came from his parents' bedroom. His father's was more of a guttural cry of rage.

Pushing against Will with a hard shove to his chest, the intruder jumped off and bolted from the bathroom, the bar coming down on his back at least once more as Will continued swinging. Scampering, the man shot for the stairs at a dead sprint and caught the strip of dental floss against his leg, tripping him as it snapped. Flipping head first down the stairway, his whole body crunched against steps as he flopped helplessly to the hardwood floor.

Will's dad got to the top of the stairs just as the man threw himself through the front door, hobbling to keep himself upright. Will was pulling himself from the tub as his father turned to look back at him. "I'm OK," was all he could manage between gasps.

His mother came running to the bathroom with the phone in hand. "It's dead," she said and dropped the phone to the floor, rushing in to throw her arms around her son.

His father bounded down the stairs, unhindered by the now broken strand of floss, charging after the man. He stopped at the bottom of the stairs. "Something's not right. I smell exhaust."

1:32 A.M.

At his father's comment about the gas, both Will and his mother ran down the stairs. They passed his father who stood in the doorway as if deciding whether to first give chase or to search for the source of the fumes.

Will's mother immediately grabbed for windows, the faux wood blinds thrapping together as she drew pull cords upward with quick yanks. Street light flooded the room illuminating the swells of swirling exhaust. Springing locks, she heaved open double-hung windows as Will moved ahead of her into the kitchen to do the same. Rectangular beams of street light glimmered into the living room.

The incoming light allowed them all to see the haunting scene filling their home. The pull of air through the open window panes sucked thinning stretches of ghostly, gray fog to the outdoors. The outdoor light lit a pathway through the clouds that were rolling in through the open garage door. Mr. Conlan turned in its direction and said, "That's coming from our car. Why would he have started it?"

Will's mind had been trying to work out the same puzzling question as he parted the drapes to another kitchen window. Using the base of his palms to shove the top frame open, he felt a cool breeze refreshingly gust against his face, clearing his mind with its briskness and allowing him to recall details he shouldn't have missed. Looking down to his waist, his eyes fell on the gas range, each burner's dial set to high. These dials had been the source of the clicks he had heard before the intruder had come up the stairs. He wondered why they had been turned on as well.

His father moved from the doorway for the first time as he stepped toward the garage. Opening the last of the living room's windows, his mother requested, "Warren, open the garage door while you're there to clear out the exhaust."

As his mother's words registered, a panic frigidly rushed through Will's entire body like opening a door to a Kwik Mart's cooler. "Dad, stop!" Will screamed out just as his father's fingers reached the push button of the wall-mounted garage opener. His hands fumbled for the stove's dials poking into his leaning waist. The dial he reached turned freely without resistance in his hand. Only now did a new odor register with his nostrils.

"Don't press it!" He ran around the refrigerator to the doorway where his dad stood frozen. Not realizing the danger they had been in until this moment, Will grabbed for his father's hand to pull it away.

"Mom, don't dare touch anything—not even a light!" he yelled back over his shoulder. He had never heard himself yell at his parents before nor had he ever given them a direct order. Their wide open eyes and sudden pause indicated they realized what he had said must be of imminent importance. Letting go of his father's hand, he urged his dad to follow behind him between the two vehicles. Will pulled on the release rope dangling from the electric garage door motor. Grabbing for the door handle, he lifted the hanging door until it rolled into its framed cradle above their heads against the textured ceiling.

"Turn off the car, but then walk across the street and wait for me. I'll be back to explain." Will ran back into the house, stopping to turn all four stove burners off. "Mom, come with me outside," he directed as he reached for his dad's cell phone from the counter top where they kept paper and supplies.

Exiting the garage, Will walked far away from the house to where his father sat on a curb. He saw his mom jog over to the neighbor's house and ring their bell to awaken them. Holding out the cell phone toward his dad he said, "We need to call the police."

"Your mother's already on it," his father replied.

It was only as he handed over the cell phone that Will noticed the baseball bat his father held against his knee and guessed he had grabbed it from the storage shelves in the garage.

Pointing at the bat, Will explained, "Hate to say it, Dad, but you about blew us up." He tried to say it in much the same light-hearted way his father had spoken to him earlier in the evening about denting the BMW. Will sat down on the front lawn beside him. "When I worked with the Red Cell, we were once shown how IEDs in Afghanistan and Iraq are often detonated by cell phones. We assumed initially that cell phones could also be used as explosive triggers in future terrorist attacks here in America.

"The deeper we got into the discussion, one man, the movie director I told you about, ranted about using other household electronic devices, claiming they could spark an explosion given the right conditions. He said that in one of his movies they considered using everything from toy car remote controls and door bells to even garage door openers. When I saw the dials on our gas stove turned on, I knew pressing that opener or anything else electronic might ignite all that gas. Our house would have most likely been blown to smithereens." Pausing to take a look at his dad, he added, "That would have definitely cost more than a dent in a BMW's door."

At this, his father gave him a long, hard look, as if really trying to decide something. "You never cease to amaze me, Will," his father replied and put his arm around his shoulder. It was about the most physical affection he'd received from his dad since their roughhousing days of his earlier childhood.

"Dad," Will said as he held out his hand, "there's one phone call I really should make."

Despite the early hour, his father didn't question the request. Holding the cell phone for him to take, he did, though, state in an even voice as he stared directly into Will's eyes, "Two attacks in one night." With those five words, Will recognized that his father had guessed who the call would be to and why. Though Will believed there was no way his parents knew of his continued work with the Analytic Red Cell, his father had put it all together. It gave him pause to consider with a growing admiration how intelligent his parents both were.

Taking the cell phone and pressing the wake button, Will was startled to see several unanswered messages. They had all come from a number he knew well. Pressing one so it would automatically redial, he shuffled away from earshot.

Standing alone, Will saw his mother walk across the driveway, the neighbor family following, all wearing robes but seemingly wide awake. He could see that they had supplied his father with a cup of warm coffee. The neighbors stood like watchmen on either side of him, his mother chattering away, still explaining the night's intrusion.

Will waited as the phone dialed Mark Tenepior. The intelligence agent answered immediately. Even before Will could speak, he heard Agent Tenepior's calm, deep voice state, "I'll be there in less than two minutes." Will heard the click and dial tone of the call's end before he was even able to speak.

Will's dad furled his eyebrows. "That didn't take long."

"Can you believe Agent Tenepior's only a few blocks away?" asked Will.

As he said this, a police car pulled against the curb. A black uniformed officer, apparently still young enough to be paying his night shift dues, stepped from the cruiser. In one hand he held a flash light, its beam highlighting a streak of grass in front of him. As he stepped up onto their lawn, he pulled a spiral-bound flip pad from his pants pocket.

But before he could even step over the sidewalk, a new, white Nissan 370Z Nismo Sports Coupe, narrowly avoiding a bumper collision, screeched to a halt behind the police car. Mark Tenepior practically jumped from the vehicle before the rev of the engine had even stopped humming. He called out, "I'll take over here."

Agent Tenepior approached the officer, his shoulders jackhammering with each authoritative stride. The officer spun around. His hand grabbed for the radio at his belt, but froze abruptly as his leveled gaze struck the massive bulk of Tenepior's chest. Fingers petrified against the radio's call button, he stood rigid for several seconds, the only movement coming from his widening eyes as they scanned Tenepior's full length and thickness of body.

Agent Tenepior opened his outstretched hand ahead of him. Ready for inspection, a Central Intelligence Agency badge nestled toylike in the folds of his huge palm. His hulking frame towered over the cop, a wall cloud squared against the night's sky.

Though Will couldn't hear their discussion, he assumed Agent Mark Tenepior was explaining his jurisdictional right to the case. Will didn't think it'd matter if the officer wanted to give up on the emergency response call or not—Tenepior always got his way. Then Will saw the most peculiar thing happen—the young officer drew his firearm. But he didn't try to point it at Agent Tenepior. Rather, he crouched down on one knee behind the shield of his police car. Arms sprawled over the hood, the young officer pointed his gun across the street.

Mark strode up to Will and asked with a nod of his head over his shoulder, "That the direction I'm assuming your housebreaker ran off to?"

Will reeled. How did Agent Tenepior realize they had been in trouble? How had he known there was an intruder? And how was he here already? Will knew that if there was anyone his father should be amazed with, it would have to be Mark Tenepior.

"That guy's dying for some action so bad that I told him I needed backup," Tenepior said in regard to the police officer. Then changing direction, he asked, "Everything all right?" He took Will by the shoulder as he nodded and led him back to where his father was seated.

Rising from the grass, his father shook the hand extended in front of him. "Glad you're here." His quick-witted greeting did not give anything away to the neighbors.

Agent Tenepior, advancing from his father's cue, asked, "Mr. Conlan, is there any place your family and I could talk privately?" implying that it was time for the neighbors to go back to their beds.

Will spoke up after the neighbors had said goodnight and his mother had thanked them in return. "Not sure if our house is safe yet."

"Gas, right?"

It was Will's parents' turn to be absolutely shocked. Though they knew all too well what this man did for a living, Will's mother couldn't help herself. "How could you have possibly known that?"

Will knew that if he had asked a question like this of Agent Tenepior a year ago in class, he'd have been berated with a perturbed response like, "You've got a head. You figure it out." But with his mother, Agent Tenepior was much more cordial and explained, "I could point out the open garage door and windows in the middle of the night as clues to impress you, but in all truth, the actual evidence came from a house fire here in Chicago several days ago. Apparently, this home was full of natural gas when the homeowner ignited the vapors by flipping a light switch. It's too much of a coincidence not to be connected and not just because of the gas. The deceased man's last name was Conlan."

"Oh my gosh," Will's mother stammered as she grabbed hold of her husband's arm.

"It is my belief," Tenepior continued on, staring directly at the two parents, "that your intruder tonight was specifically targeting your son."

1:48 A.M.

It was Will's father who asked Agent Tenepior the first question. He did so without denial or alarm in his voice. "So do you know who this guy is?"

Only Will noticed Tenepior blink. He assumed it was shocking to find a parent utterly accept his son being targeted by an apparent assassin. Most parents would completely freak out at the accusation. Born on a ranch, his father had seen his fair share of difficult situations to work through. Will figured he must have already worked out the truth of the story for himself so his father had been prepared for it.

"Not entirely," Agent Tenepior explained. "I'll explain when we get to the substation. It's a secure area and we can talk freely there."

"We're going to the substation?" asked Will's mother.

"I ordered a team to assemble and make their way here. They will make sure your home is safe and collect specific items you feel you'll need and bring them to us. Warren, I want you and your wife to follow Will and me there in your car. Now that your location has been compromised, we'll need to keep you under our protection for the time being. I'll answer any questions you have when we get there." He paused, seeming to consider anything he may have missed. "And, Katherine, don't worry about your charity event. We'll send escorts to go along so you can still attend."

Once again, Will's mother looked at him with utter dismay. Will knew that she'd be working on that one for a while. He guessed that when they got to the CIA substation, his mother's first question would be to ask how *he* seemed to know as much about her own family as she did. Will only hoped that none of it was breaking some invasion of privacy law since he was pretty sure that when she found out he was still working with the Analytic Red Cell behind their backs that Agent Tenepior might need more than his combat training to hold her off.

These thoughts were still running through Will's mind as he shut the car door of Agent Tenepior's new Nissan behind him. "How fast can this go?" he asked, but was actually being rhetorical. "You may need it to get away from Mom if she finds out we still work together."

"I'd put money on it that your dad already knows."

At that, Will wondered if his parents had given Agent Tenepior as much to figure out as he had given them.

"And if he doesn't," Tenepior continued on, "I'm afraid that's going to be unavoidable now. He'll have it worked out that I got to the scene way faster than I should have by the time we get to headquarters."

"And how did you?" Will wanted to know.

"Will, you may not realize how important you are to our agency or what we do. The second your home alarm was disabled, we were notified. After all, it is our system."

"I thought we were secured by Eagle Eye."

"Check the billing address sometime—I think you'll recognize it. In any case, a full disarming of the system specially installed in your home was a sure sign of foul play. Since we had just talked, I tried our video link, but it didn't work either. I was in my car and on the phone within seconds, trying to call your dad's cell. Remind me to either talk your parents into getting you a cell phone or I'll get one for you."

Will pieced bits of what Agent Tenepior said together, "So you knew about the other Conlan and didn't tell me?" He felt slightly betrayed since they had talked just before the intrusion.

"Forensics on this other Conlan showed there were physical signs of torture before his house burst into flames. This indicated that his attacker hadn't gone for the instant kill. Since the only connection to you was his last name, the agency was willing to call it a coincidence. That all changed when you and your friends were attacked earlier this evening. Since then, every spare agent has been working on his identity and who he could be affiliated with." Agent Tenepior paused as if weighing his thoughts. He spoke much slower when he continued. "We were too confident in the measures we've taken to protect you and keep your identity secret. We all truthfully agreed there was no way he could find or get to you before you joined us for our Red Team session in the morning."

Will knew Tenepior had chosen his words carefully. What he hadn't said was that he hadn't wanted to "alarm" Will. Agent Tenepior had gone out of his way to not treat Will like a child. But why, then, had he kept Will in the dark about his attacker?

"After ending our conversation, I considered the police report. Those don't always get filed immediately and I knew we wouldn't get your address erased from the report until the police offices opened the next morning. So, I decided to play it safe and send a car to stake out your house. But before I could even order it, we were alerted that your security system was disconnected. That's when I left here."

This time as they pulled into the CIA substation, there were no secret entrances or hidden elevators. It wasn't likely that a fifteen-year-old boy would be spotted entering in the dead of night. They simply passed through the guarded gate and parked near a side entrance.

The gray brick building was nothing fancy on the outside. Fitting the clandestine nature of the CIA, the building's bland appearance camouflaged it against other warehouse buildings down the street. Rather than bullying its way across an entire city block, it nestled its square frame of a protective big brother into a quiet industrial area. If it weren't for the fence topped with razor wire and the armed guard at the gate post, no one would suspect anything unusual about the place.

The interior, on the other hand, was pretentiously decorated with high-end office furniture and the latest equipment. A gigantic screen surrounded by tinier clusters of LED panels on both sides filled the center of the main operation's hall, each desk and cubicle positioned so these could be seen with a minor swivel of a chair. Several halos of lamp light dotted the sectionals, marking the attendants who were working late into the night breaking down intelligence or monitoring national security concerns. The crest of the CIA was etched into the tile at the center of the enormous open room and into the glass of Mark Tenepior's office.

Tenepior took a seat in a leather chair behind a new mahogany desk after entering the office. Will's family followed in behind. A large conference table lay before them, long enough for the sixteen chairs pushed into positions around the table. Will, immediately making himself at home, pulled out a couple of chairs and plopped himself between the two, throwing his feet up on the second. His parents, exhausted at the late hour and too overwhelmed by their surroundings to remain standing, took seats on the couch behind Tenepior's desk, Will's mother lying against his father's chest as she leaned back into him.

Will could see his mother was gathering strength from his dad's embrace just before she broke the silence, "So what is it that you *do* know about the man who broke into our home tonight?" Though Will could see how tired she was, his parents weren't going to rest until they got a few answers. They were, after all, sitting in a command post belonging to the world's most renowned intelligence agency.

"Logic would tell us that he's connected to the terrorists Will disposed of last year, but even that's a stretch since the only ones to know of Will are all either in the custody of Homeland Security or have been eliminated for their crimes." The words were spat as if they had left a bad taste in his mouth. Will could tell that Agent Tenepior didn't like not having the answers. "What we do know for sure is that he's very capable with a computer. It's usually China we have to worry about with cyber security, but there's not a single reason to believe they would have cause to target Will. Because of this and that the two attacks were by the same person, the assumption is we are dealing with a single individual with incredible hacking skills. We've closely monitored any online personal information about Will to the point where he's virtually invisible to the prying eye. Yet this attacker still managed to locate your son tonight through a post on his friend Ryan's Facebook account."

Will's father's arm squeezed his wife's shoulders tighter. The strain of her eyes showed as much concern as the quavering in her voice as she asked, "Is that how he found our home?"

"One possibility is that he found Will through the two of you. Perhaps one of your employers mentioned your names on a webpage that we haven't intercepted and altered yet. Tonight's police report is another likely option. He may have hacked the police database. It reasons that he hadn't located any information prior to Ryan's Facebook post. Attacks tend to be more planned out than just simple kidnappings or muggings. It looks like he took advantage of the moment."

Will's mother stared up into his father's face, her chin rising toward his. Only a few hours remained until sunup and they all had tired streaks under their eyes. Will could tell from the long pause of silence that they'd sensed they'd get no further and decided to give the questions a rest until morning.

Just as they were falling back asleep, a young man wearing thick, black-framed glasses ran into Tenepior's office and shouted with urgency, "You gotta see this!"

Waking with a start, both Will's parents sprang from the couch, pouncing to the floor with bent knees almost as if they had automatically readied themselves for another break-in. Will was much more casual with his reaction as he merely rolled his head sideways to look at the person who had barged into the office.

Motioning for them all to come into the main operation hall with a wave of his arm, the young man swiveled, his thin black tie flopping over his shoulder in his haste. Will wondered why he was wearing a tie at night.

"What is it, Joe?" Tenepior asked.

Will realized they wouldn't have been bothered if the information didn't somehow pertain to tonight's events, and stood from his chair to follow.

Joe began pressing a remote's button to initialize the big screen into showing what he had found on his desktop computer. Within a few seconds, the beams of light that shot out from the projector displayed a black square with a triangle play button at the bottom left corner.

After the clip had finished spooling, an image of a man standing at the edge of a balcony with a noose hung about his neck appeared. The simple, white-plastered room below him was full of men all clothed in what unmistakably had to be of Middle Eastern fashion. Immediately Will wondered what this recording had to do with almost getting gassed out of his own home.

Then the image seemed to focus more on the condemned man than the crowd of witnesses as it zoomed in to reveal the anguish tormenting his face, a look of distress Will recognized all too immediately. Though it had been very dark when he had first locked eyes on the man, his look of agony was unmistakable. Will had spent numerous nights awake in bed shivering at the year-old memory of this man trying to kill him. It was one of many nightmares he often relived from that experience. The luminescent numbers of the bomb strapped across Will's chest still vibrantly ticked backward in his mind; the man's threats to blow Will's body to bits often stirred his wakefulness.

But it was that one undeniable look of pain that made Will certain of his identity. This was one of the terrorists that helped Es Sayid attack the CIA substation last year. That grimace was equally burned into Will's memory each time he recalled kicking a dead drop spike through the man's thigh to free himself from this man's hold. Once marking Will's triumph, the man's tortured expression now felt surprisingly ill-fated.

"That's...It's..." Will's voice trailed off as he pointed up at the screen unable to complete his statement since he'd never known the man's name. His parents stared at him, their open-mouthed expressions showing how bewildered they were that their son could possibly have been exposed to such harsh realities of world conflict that he was viewing this clip with intrigue, not disgust.

"Umar Ghazi," Tenepior muttered at the same time as if trying to piece together the video's relevance aloud to himself.

The clip ran its length. Umar's venomous ranting echoed throughout the open room. As the shrieking of his dying words were cut from his throat, Will's mother cried out as her trembling hand immediately went to her mouth. Her cries were as barefaced as her disbelief that the executed man had known her son.

Agent Tenepior's easy nature with his mother from earlier in the evening seemed to vanish as he didn't turn to comfort or to assure her, but instead to question Joe, his mind already at work on the necessary steps to take. "That video still live?"

"We're forcing the provider to remove it from their network as we speak."

"How long's it been searchable?"

"735 hits; the last few being ours. It appears to have been active since the day of his execution in August."

"I want to know the name and IP address of anyone who's viewed it along with the individuals responsible for its posting. And stop all routing traffic to that IP as well!" Agent Tenepior turned in a new direction and yelled an order across the operations hall as he pointed up at the projection screen. "I want a list of everyone who was present for that execution. I need to know every name in that room!"

"Already on it," announced another agent two desks over. "Facial recognition software has already ID'd four of the guards on the balcony. If the data's right, every one of them has been reported dead within the last few weeks."

In deep thought, Agent Tenepior's gaze sunk to his shoes. He looked up sharply at Will's mother. "Katherine, this may actually be good. If we can track down the rest of these people, we'll have a narrowed list of suspects and know who we are dealing with. Singular, targeted killings are typically the work of murderers, not organized terrorist groups. Thus, we most likely have a single person operating independently. Locate him and we can put a stop to it all."

Then, pacing as he stared at the floor, Tenepior continued to speak. "The larger issue is we can't foresee what impact the video has had. Though it's far from viral, it most likely has been spreading at an enormous rate through radical communities. I'm sure some viewers were simply humored by Umar's ungraceful wailing or even intrigued by his inescapable predicament. What worries me more are the viewers who have taken silent notice, nodding their heads, a faraway look in their eyes.

"The victim's words could have rubbed salt into some intangible, festering wound they feel in their lives—a lesion opened by the loss of many basic freedoms denied to them by American foreign policy. This fallacious ache, they could come to believe, may only be eased through retaliation against any American, especially one they can now call by name."

8:00 A.M.

The hectic sounds of a room teeming with people stirred Will from his sleep. So busy in their tasks, they didn't even notice him as he groggily shuffled past on his way to the shower room. Though he turned the shower's dial to high, chilly sprinkles of water drizzled his back and shocked his body back into consciousness. It was a rudely fitting conclusion to the bedless night that had stiffened his back and spoon-fed him disturbing dreams.

After lightly toweling off, he stepped his dripping toes into the corridor's hallway. He hoped he could remain as unobserved now as he made his way to the prison wing with only a bath towel around his waist. Wishing he had done this before showering, he shuffled down long hallways looking for the room his family's clothes had been brought to late last night. Fittingly, they'd placed his entire wardrobe in an unoccupied prison chamber, shirts hanging from a chin-up bar and the iron railings of the cell.

Flipping through the hanging clothes brought from his home, his hand rested on his purple Northwestern Wildcat hoodie. It wasn't one he wore a lot, but being from Chicago, it was natural for him to root for the home team, often visiting Ryan Field in Evanston for a fall football game with his father.

It struck him as funny that hanging right next to the Wildcat sweatshirt was a Nebraska Cornhusker t-shirt. Before the 2011 football season, it wouldn't have mattered much, but Nebraska had joined the Big 10 Conference that year and was grouped into the same division as Northwestern, adding them to their regular season schedule. This turned out to be a blessing as Will could now watch his favorite two teams play each other once a year. Rooting for the Huskers had always been natural for Will since his parents had met at the University of Nebraska. His family made a Saturday habit of wearing red and watching the Husker game on TV. He immediately grabbed the shirt that proudly proclaimed GO BIG RED in big block letters and pulled the red fabric over his head. After all, he figured, he was on his way to attend a session with the Analytic Red Cell. He might as well dress the part.

Will met his father exiting Agent Tenepior's office. "More bad news this morning," his father announced. "The gun recovered from our bathroom was untraceable. And the only fingerprints not blotted out by globs of shampoo yielded no matches."

"You have to admit the shampoo was still a pretty *suave* move," Will joked.

His father rolled his eyes and changed the subject. "I was informed there's a break room with a TV around here. Apparently it's the only option for me until your meeting ends."

"That what Agent Tenepior told you?"

"Must not be suave enough to participate," replied Will's dad facetiously. "What he actually said, more or less, is that this ol' cowboy's not been invited to the rodeo."

Though he wished his dad could see firsthand his involvement with the Red Cell, he had to smirk at the offhand comment. Part of his dad's charm had always been his grass roots upbringing. "Country" sayings like this often escaped his lips to reinforce an understated point.

Will had never quite forgiven him for asking if he needed "a little more lead in his pencil" within earshot of his teammates after slapping a weak grounder back to the pitcher in a tournament ballgame. Any mention of "taking out a pencil" from a teacher in school since then elicited immature giggles from his buddy Kyle. He humorously had to bear the butt of a joke later that baseball season when returning to the dugout after striking out to find each of his fun-loving teammates with a pencil stuck behind their right ears. Even if a different approach would have been more tactful, his dad usually got his argument across.

"Dad, I don't think they allow anyone to know what we discuss while Red Teaming. Part of that whole 'Top Secret' business. All those guys have to sign nondisclosure agreements saying they won't tell anyone. And besides, today we aren't going to be in that office for long. The whole group's leaving to visit some target site."

"Still can't believe my terrorist-fighting, fifteen-year-old son helps some of the country's brightest minds to secure the entire nation. Could you at least see if they'd help figure out how to protect our own home?"

"We tend to concentrate on things that would cause a little more wide-spread panic, Dad. But I'll let you know if anything comes up."

"No, but really, what do you talk about? Give your dad a hint. How do *you* help?"

"Dad, what I can tell you is we try to figure out a terrorist's next move before he makes it. And for some reason, I've been very good at helping them do this. No one else was able to figure out their use of Treks commercials to communicate and coordinate attacks. If there's a weakness in our defenses like that, they'd like my help finding it before the bad guys do."

"You have always been a remarkable kid, Will. You have a gift of vision, whether it's eyeing a pitcher's throw or knowing what girl to date. But this business deals with terrorists who are hateful and sneaky. I guess what I'm trying to say is that if you're going to be a part of all this, you need to remember that cows will always find the open gate."

Will stood there a moment and simply stared back at his dad. His advice held such meaning and caution. Maybe it was his way of saying to be careful, or even to make sure he's thorough. As it sunk in, he thought maybe Agent Tenepior was wrong about not allowing his dad to participate in the Red Cell's discussions. He seemed to see as clearly as any of them.

Not fully aware of how to respond, he turned to open the door to Agent Tenepior's office, the room where local Red Teaming sessions began.

No sooner had Will pulled back the chair he had slept in last night at the long table, when a gray-bearded man in his fifties wearing a tweed jacket entered the room. Will had never met the man before. Agent Tenepior rose from his desk to greet the new participant. "Will, I'd like you to meet Dr. Winthrop, a professor of explosives engineering who's here today to help us prepare against bombings." It was clear that the professor was stunned to have a teenager included in a clandestine Homeland Security operation. His disapproving scowl said it all. Will could immediately tell this made the man worried his time would be wasted.

"I was brought here to speak to kids?" the man accused.

Agent Tenepior slapped Will on the shoulder before turning back to his desk. "Will, why don't you tell Dr. Winthrop about the improvised explosive you encountered last night at your home."

The annoyance of the professor's frown curled into a challenging grin of skepticism. "You have some experience with explosives, do you?" It was clear the explosives engineer was a serious man who handled unrelenting situations and was not to be bothered by some teenager who couldn't possibly understand the nature of his "one mistake and you're dead" world. He probably thought Will was some misguided trouble-maker who experimented with building pipe bombs.

Equally irritated, Will retorted, "I was once told that a shock wave of exploding C-4 would shoot through my guts at five miles a second." Will allowed a small smile to creep onto his face as he nonchalantly continued, "I stabbed the guy before he could prove it."

The comment seemed to have the desired effect. An open mouth replaced the professor's grin. He inadvertently gripped his briefcase tighter against his chest with his forearm. "You stabbed someone last night?" he stammered with uncertainty.

"No. The man I stabbed has been dead for months. Last night I only managed to burn the guy."

The professor exhaled sharply. Will thought he looked faint.

Will could tell from his raised eyebrows and the shift of his eyes between them that Agent Tenepior was enjoying the exchange. Otherwise, he knew he would have been cut off before he could talk back. It was probably vindicating for the agent to see his star pupil holding his own. Will wondered if he could still somehow wisecrack about blowing up cars, but thought it better not to bring that up again.

Before he could make up his mind, other professionals who had been asked to join the Red Team started walking through the office door, many walking over to give Will greetings of handshakes before taking their seats. The professor just stood there looking dismayed.

Agent Tenepior introduced each of the participants and acknowledged the distinct expertise that each individual could offer, skipping his description of only Will by simply stating he was "uniquely fitted" for his role with the Red Cell.

Agent Tenepior addressed the entire room. "There has been a growing trend for extremists to target highly crowded public areas. Their mission is to also create widespread psychological fear, and, in effect, add additional burden to our country's frail economy with additional loss of potential revenue.

"We have challenged our initial assumptions about such possible soft target attacks in prior Red Cell sessions. You can further investigate these critiques in the past Red Cell reports I've copied and placed on your tables for you to read. We feel this group can further expand on those possibilities and determine yet more slants to consider.

"We'll start with a list of likely potential 'soft' targets, but, as always, you can formulate other possibilities. We would also like you to devise probable means of attacks; play out any situation that could cause a massive loss of life.

"Let's break into three groups of four. The first group will plan an attack on a tourist attraction. Group two will focus on a shopping center. Number three, you'll get a sporting venue. As always, when we work with our models, do not shy away from any possibility no matter how remote you think they realistically may be. 'Not likely' shouldn't be a part of your discussions. Leave that to the Intelligence officials within the Agency to discuss their plausibility afterward. Let's see what you come up with."

RED CELL REPORT
APPLYING ALTERNATIVE ANALYSIS TO HOMELAND SECURITY

Soft Targets: The "Flesh Effect"

February 3, 2008

CLASSIFIED

Summary

Soft targets are relatively unprotected sites with little or no military protection. The more security measures added to symbolic targets, the more likely soft targets will attract terrorist plots. Though a homegrown attack could zero in on any target, an event that accumulates a mass of people numbering 10,000 should be considered within the sights of international terrorists.

Focus

An attack that creates casualties (coined as the "Flesh Effect") is more likely to be planned. As a result, this session concentrated on highly populated entertainment venues (i.e., amusement parks, state fairs, concerts, stadiums). Less populated soft targets such as oil drilling sites, power stations, government buildings, and ethanol plants were not considered within this discussion.

Challenging Security Beliefs

If predictable, attacks can be prevented; therefore, terrorists think atypically. Red Cells are charged with challenging conventional ideas to expose unforeseen possibilities.

Initial Assumption: *To be a success, an attack on a soft target must result in a large number of casualties.* While a high body count would be an attack's main priority, Red Teamers believe opportunities to create fear, economic disruption, or publicity are enough to provoke an attack.

Initial assumption: *It's about the event, not the site.* Unlike 9/11's symbolic and economical choices of high-profile hard targets, entertainment venues are targeted for the mass of people. These events may become windfalls since high value targets (i.e., dignitaries, celebrities, political figures) are often in attendance and additional casualties would be created.

Initial Assumption: *Bombs are the most probable threat.* Aircraft flying above or automobiles traveling to a stadium could be exploited to spread chemical/ biological weapons. By hacking video displays, propaganda or martyrdom could be promoted. Disguised as vendors, terrorists could conduct preoperational surveillance for months and have clearance to bring supplies inside a site.

Recommendations

- Run background checks on all facilities' vendors
- Install cameras at all access points and compare images against terrorist lists
- Train staff to spot unusual activity (e.g., people loitering, filming exits, counting steps)
- Do not publish facility blueprints
- Randomly alter venue delivery entrances and security patrols
- Increase baggage and body checks and restrict outside beverage containers

9:20 A.M.

Will had participated in one other "model" session in his last year of Red Teaming. He knew the participants would be equipped with three-dimensional models as well as blueprints of floor plans and even video footage of the specific targets on individual laptops. The last time, he got to mess around with an authentic replica of a nuclear power plant the size of a pool table that he could take apart and see all the inner chambers all the way down to the reactor itself. He had found it handy to be able to manipulate pieces to find weak points and potential security risks.

Taking a seat, Will grabbed a laptop from his group's table and stared at the question that was pulsing on the screen: "If you were a terrorist, how would you target a crowded shopping center?" It was to be the guiding force in their brainstorming, research, and discussion. After being analyzed by intelligence personnel within Homeland Security, their answer, he knew, would become the foundation for a report that would guide related venues in establishing and strengthening prevention and response procedures.

A young web penetration tester who had joined Will in the second group believed that their mock attack should focus on the superstore's ventilation system. Making sport of their brainstorms, this breakthrough came from lively but brief considerations of arson, bomb planting, tampering with hand sanitizer and soap dispensers, and a very wild idea about releasing malaria-infested swarms of mosquitoes inside the building. The pen tester swiped the laptop from Will, as he was an expert in using technology to breach systems, and used the cursor to point out the HVAC (heating, ventilation & air conditioning) ductwork on the roof of the mall displayed on his laptop screen. "We release a gas agent into their air intake which will spread throughout the building and wipe out everyone inside. It's unguarded, unwatched by any cameras, and flat roofs tend to easily hide things from the view below."

Coordinating the discussion for the group, an intelligence officer directed operational questions to each of the group members based on his or her field of expertise. Since it was well known among all the intelligence operatives that Will had broken into this very CIA substation a year ago and successfully outmaneuvered six armed terrorists in the process, the officer drilled Will about how to best access the air ducts built into the roof. Will poured over a 360-degree viewing of the mall on the laptop, searching for anything that could be overlooked, never taking his eyes from the screen as they talked. He spotted several shady corners where bushes had grown too tall, concealing spots from the view of traffic where a person could climb his way up.

From the corner of his eye, Will noticed a white-haired man had entered the office and was shuffling among the groups listening in on their conversations. He steadied each step by leaning on a cane. "Einstein!" Will called out and waved his hand for the man to come over as he stood to meet him half way.

Though the intelligence officer's hair matched that of the great physicist, Einstein's nickname had actually come from how he compared with the world-renowned scientist in intellect. He had spent his entire career as an intelligence officer and was regarded as one who had both the resources and brains to manipulate any situation to his favor. There was even a rumor told in hushed whispers about how his intel had secretly led to the entire elimination of at least two organized terrorist groups.

"What has your group come up with?" he asked Will out of the corner of his mouth.

"Ventilation system."

He whispered back, "You didn't come up with that idea, did you?" Einstein's suggestion sounded to Will more like a statement than a question. "Almost like a bad movie plot, isn't it? I'd have figured you to follow your teenage stomach to the food court for a plot to kill everyone," he stated dryly.

Suddenly recalling his report from last night about poisoning food, Will gave Einstein a double take. How in the world did the man predict that his plot idea would involve food as he had suggested in his paper just the night before? It had been a complete Tenepior-esque observation. "How did you..?"

"Oh, don't get your boxers in a bunch." He tossed a stapled pile of folded notebook paper down on Will's lap that he had removed from his back pocket. "I read your school report that you were writing after we swiped it from your home last night."

Will was relieved. He thought that it would have been entirely freaky if Einstein could have been able to predict such a thing. There would have been no explaining it.

"What'd you think?" Will asked, earnestly wanting to know if his terror proposal would meet the senior CIA official's approval.

"Food terrorism is a serious concern, one that might create a devastating attack. The World Health Organization acknowledged the threat food poses as a potential medium for distributing such biological and chemical agents to the public very early on in our fight against terrorism. We've had several Red Cells discuss the matter in the past."

Agent Tenepior began walking toward the two of them.

Einstein continued, "I like your idea about adding cyanide to the water you cook hotdogs in, but cooking it in extreme temperatures deactivates the poison, so that wouldn't work. There was a similar idea about slipping cyanide or ricin into salad bars that we uncovered a few years back. Overall it's good enough for a school report, but not for here." Einstein paused and looked at Agent Tenepior before shaking his head. "I don't think it could be carried out the way you've proposed. In either case, the topic's been covered."

Adding finality to his statement, Einstein turned to shuffle off to listen in on the next group. His response puzzled and irritated Will. It wasn't like him or anyone in the Red Cell to discourage ideas. He thought it especially unusual when an idea like his was so plausible. In fact, Will was pretty sure if he had the right materials he could carry out such an attack on his own.

Now that he and Agent Tenepior were standing alone, Will nodded toward Einstein and asked, "What's bothering him?"

Placing a hand on his shoulder in a moment of warmth that was rare for the man, Tenepior said, "It's not you. For one thing, he didn't get any sleep last night. After learning of the assault on you, he came here to frantically work the night through. He seems to be personally taking it upon himself to do something about your attacker."

They both watched as Einstein milled around a circle of chairs, his head leaning in to catch the discussion as he bent his waist forward. He pointed to a stack of papers and appeared to plant an idea as he spoke to the group. With his single suggestion, they could overhear him steering the conversation into a new direction. His examination had been quick and on target.

Turning away from Einstein's direction to face Will, Tenepior began speaking again. "It definitely doesn't do him any good that he has to work under me. If I didn't hold this position, he would." And as if he'd been reflecting on the matter for some time, Agent Tenepior continued, "He's probably better on his own, but when I was promoted above him, I ignored his unwillingness to take direction from me because I wanted him on my team. Between you and me, he resents his body and blames it for holding back his career. It didn't help any that he and I were the lead strategists in an unsuccessful campaign to defend Chicago last year. He had done everything humanly possible to discover Es Sayid's plots. With each attack that occurred, the more heat we took. Our tactics took different paths and when mine found you, we got our big breakthrough.

"You've got to understand that failure is especially hard for a man of his talent. As you well know, success in our business is not easy. So, with little regard to its risks, he exhausts himself working on his own to filter any irrational muck into reasonable intelligence. Not everyone can say they are the best at what they do. It is quite difficult for people like him who are the best and receive the criticism but not the recognition."

"I'm sorry," Will said gloomily, "but that doesn't excuse him from treating my idea like dirt. I appreciate the help, but I worked hard on that plot."

"Is this the paper you had to rewrite?"

"That's the one. It's an I-search on planning the perfect terror attack."

"And what kind of attack would that be?"

"Apparently, not a good one," Will stated flatly, his eyes never looking away from Einstein.

In response, Agent Tenepior simply patted the top of his shoulder a few times and walked away.

Because he knew Einstein's insight would be valuable to his report, Will decided to follow him to where Group Three was seated. Relying on Dr. Winthrop's expertise, his group had been discussing the use of hydrogen peroxide-based explosives to attack a stadium or arena. Immediately engrossed in the topic, Will stepped closer. The professor was adamantly shaking his head with impatience. It seemed as if teenagers weren't the only ones subject to his pompous indignation.

"No, no, no. It would be much simpler than that. These explosives aren't that hard to make," Dr. Winthrop's voice was full of exasperation— as if he had not already explained it for the hundredth time. "Don't you guys remember the Tang Bomb back in 2006—how terrorists were going to blow up planes by using that orange drink as a catalyst for the hydrogen peroxide?"

Though he had been speaking to very intelligent professionals, it was clear that none of them had more than a Fourth of July's experience with explosives and weren't piecing together his point. But from behind him, Will did. He had focused a great deal of time and energy participating in sports and attending sporting events, and he had seen all too easily the horrifying possibilities hidden within the professor's message.

"So they wouldn't catch anybody at the entry gate baggage check if the things needed to make the bomb were already located inside the stadium," concluded Will.

"Exactly!" shouted the professor with obvious glee that someone finally understood. He turned around to see who had grasped what he was saying. His eyes clearly showed the shock of finding that it had come from the fifteen-year-old, Will.

"Hydrogen peroxide is a cleaning solution, right?" Will asked with a little hesitancy, trying to explain how he'd put it all together. As usual, he possessed the innate ability to spot clues and draw conclusions. It was the same skill that first attracted the CIA's attention. He was simply able to see things differently from most others. "Well, surely there would be some in a janitor's closet or even the training facility as an antiseptic. Players wouldn't be drinking anything as sugary as Tang, but a stadium would have loads of energy drink mixes or even sugar from cotton candy stands to serve as the explosive's fuel. No one would get caught smuggling in a bomb if it could be made while inside."

Worried expressions grew on the faces of each group member with the realization of just how easy it might be for terrorist chaos to bring the United States to its knees. The professor stood and placed his hand on Will's shoulder. "Well, there's probably too much salt in Gatorade for a reaction to happen, but, yes, the basic premise of what he says is possible since the other ingredients needed could be mixed from household chemicals also found in the stadium." He faced the group as he spoke, but began to pat the top of Will's shoulder with an excited reassurance as he explained his point.

Will felt as if he had just received a compliment. He gauged that this man's deep enthusiasm for his field was so intense that it immediately overshadowed any skepticism he had felt earlier. It looked as if the professor had finally found an ally with whom he could openly share and discuss his passion.

Einstein chose this moment to announce the shuttles were ready to take them all to their next destination. "Phase two of today's Red Cell proceedings will be onsite. One of my colleagues or I will explain more once we get boarded."

Will quickly excused himself for a restroom break before going out to the shuttle. Still chapped about Einstein's disregard of his school report's topic, Will decided the soft target they were going to visit might provide the perfect opportunity to prove his point.

Instead of going to the restroom, he turned the corner and ran to the break room. Opening the door, he quickly looked past his seated father to see if there really was a coffee maker on the counter. As he'd hoped, his memory was correct. He knew he would find what he needed there. Just moments before, the professor had unintentionally given Will an idea. He wasn't sure if he'd find any chemicals at their destination, but there would more than likely be vast quantities of other potential supplies that Will now planned to utilize.

11:00 A.M.

As he jogged to the shuttles that would transport them to their study site, Will considered how the Red Cell participants often toured specific targets to get a better idea of how an attack could transpire. The hands-on experience of opening closed doors and casing security systems often produced more ideas than would have been gained from sitting in a conference room. Small details became evident that wouldn't be shown on some blueprint or diagram. How furniture is arranged or where a dumpster is placed could mean all the difference to someone planning an attack. He had often been reminded by Einstein that there's not as much to gain from a picture of the Sistine Chapel as standing in the very room and gazing up at Michelangelo's remarkable ceiling.

If Will had a choice, he hoped their trip would focus on Group Three's topic. He'd love to make a journey to a stadium like Soldier Field. It'd be a real kick to get a personal tour of the locker rooms and the third floor United Club. His favorite, Wrigley Field, would be even better, but he knew the Cubs had a series at home this weekend so he doubted they'd visit the historic ballpark. Their purpose was to envision the possibilities within a location, not test the actual security in place. That was left for trained CIA agents to check. Those agents could deal with the hassle of real-life crowds and security hovering over them.

Einstein turned in his front cushioned shuttle seat to face the six other participants. "For today's second session, we will be role playing attack scenarios at a local cinema."

Will's heart sank a little because he could go to a theater any day.

"For those of you who haven't been involved with the Red Cell before, we like to get you in action so you will acquire a better understanding of just how an attacker would operate and proceed. You will pretend you are the assailants and act out your plots for our viewing. The entire theater is at our disposal, so you may use anything to your advantage. Rely on your expertise to find destructive means that security measures haven't prepared for. We want to find the weak plates in their armor."

Will sat with Tobias, the web penetration tester, who he had steadily befriended during the day. Their friendly competition of trying to best each other's creative ideas during the brainstorming session had now transformed into to debating everything from college football playoffs to the best James Bond movie of all time. Where Tobias could name most of the Bond girls and Will each movie's villain, they both agreed their favorite parts were the high-tech gadgets.

This discussion reminded Will of why they were going to the theater. Since this was Tobias's first Red Teaming session, Will pointed out, "The trick to role playing is to either be very sneaky or use something as a prop in a unique way. Ultimately, it's best if you could pull off both." He knew these CIA guys who lived in the world of spies and espionage loved seeing the James Bond sleight of hand where a toothpick and straw are turned into a lethal blowgun.

After arriving at the multiplex, they divided into two groups as separated by the shuttles. Each had been allowed to browse around the cinema before gathering again with his group in either the entrance area or one of the auditoriums. Will rested in a high-back recliner seat as his group began searching for places where a bomb could be concealed. They fiddled with the giant draping curtains for a spot to hide their pretend device and even looked behind the screen. One man kept tinkering with the space beneath the seats and another examined the trash receptacles at the entrance of the auditorium. Will played along where he could, finding the most practicality in the hidden nature of the trash bins. He reasoned the bins wouldn't be emptied until the end of the movie and were ideally concealed by both darkness and in-wall wooden storage units. At one point, he pretended to smuggle a bomb under his Husker shirt. Pulling an improvised cardboard drink carrier from underneath the red tee, he dropped it into the bottom of a trash container at the entrance of the theater and pretended to exit without seeing the movie.

After their role play, his group gathered at the top of the stairs to peek inside the projection room. Will decided to excuse himself for a break. When he returned a few minutes later holding a cardboard carrier full of popcorn bags, he found his group back in the front row of seats discussing new schemes.

Einstein gave Will a hard look about what he brought back with him.

"What?" Will challenged. "You said anything was at our disposal. And my mind needs to dispose of a little of this to think."

He handed a bag of popcorn to each of his group members. Even Einstein relented and took one. While popping a kernel into his mouth, the musician of the group offered the thought that the speakers could be tampered with to blast at such a loud decibel as to burst peoples' ear drums. A software programmer was interested in the possibility of nefarious subliminal messages being added to the commercial ads before the movie.

As they were discussing a unique idea about sprinkling chemical, biological or radiological (CBR) materials on the seat cushions, the second group joined them in the auditorium. Will jumped up to offer each of them a bag of popcorn. Between mouthfuls, they began to describe potential weak points in the cinema's security measures. The harder they assessed these vulnerabilities, the more evident the site's strengths became. The shortcomings Will's small group had discussed no longer seemed like plausible attack possibilities.

For one, the spreading of CBR materials on the cushions would be very hazardous and might be detected by smells, residues, or stains. Also, the speakers of a theater didn't produce enough decibels of loud sound to kill anyone. In particular, Dr. Winthrop thought there would be too many variables for a bomb plot. "Most explosives are too unstable and difficult to detonate to just throw in the trash. It'd also be too hard to gauge chemical reaction times."

The appearance of relief stretched across each of the group member's faces. One could tell by their relaxing shoulders that they thought maybe it wasn't as easy as previously believed to plan an attack and kill everyone there. "If security precautions remain reasonable, I think our efforts today, apart from a suicide bomber, have proven that an attack would either be intercepted or wouldn't likely result in a massive loss of life," spoke a philosopher who seemed to have it all figured out. Several red teamers nodded their heads in agreement.

"Then we haven't thought hard enough," disagreed a frustrated Einstein as he shook his head the opposite direction. "Colonel Mustard here," he accused as he lifted a finger toward the philosopher, "doesn't get the luxury of digging through a stack of Clue cards when he works for us. Our Red

Cell's mission is to figure out the murder weapon even *before* Mr. Boddy gets attacked." Einstein exhaled and waved a hand dismissively in the air. "You all seem convinced there's no way to kill every person in this room."

"I managed to do it."

They all immediately looked at the fifteen-year-old who had plopped down on the stage beneath the screen, his feet dangling in front of him as he continued to shove popcorn into his mouth. Will playfully managed a quick sinister pinch to his eyes that he flashed toward Einstein before he continued. He had been waiting all morning to prove the original plan of his school report was well thought out and completely conceivable.

After taking his time to chew and swallow, Will began, "I'm glad everyone enjoyed the popcorn I snagged from the concessions. I personally thought mine was a little bland, but that's probably because I took special care in salting all yours." Reaching into his pocket and pulling out one of the unused pink sugar packets he had smuggled in from the CIA substation's break room as a prop, he slapped it down on the stage's edge. "Cyanide can be *particularly* nasty," he said not taking his eyes off the packets.

Then, feeling that he had to further explain, he slid off the stage and faced the group. "Everyone naturally assumes the concessions are safe to eat. Why would anyone think differently? And this is why it's the perfect way to attack unsuspecting movie watchers. The plan's so simple, it'd be easy to carry out. Wouldn't take much to coordinate dozens or even hundreds of people to tamper with or swap out a condiment shaker or two in theaters all over the country on a given night. Heck, this intelligent group of people fell for it. You've all been happily munching on your own bags of the stuff. And pretty soon, you'll all be dead."

Will was smiling as he finished, but Dr. Winthrop was not. Now sweating, he immediately jumped up clutching his stomach, looking as if he were about to barf. The professor seemed to have reason to believe that Will was truly capable of such a bad thing. With a heave, his hand went to his mouth, covering inflated cheeks as he bent away from the onlookers, his astonished peers gawking at how such a weak stomach didn't fit the man's steel nerves. Apparently, he was the only one who didn't realize that Will, like a true Red Teamer, was simply still role playing.

For Immediate Release
Neutrogenacide

Summary
Exposure to a chemical can occur by breathing it, absorbing it through skin, or eating foods that contain it. To enact a widespread attack, terrorists would most likely spread chemical agents through water sources or food supplies, though many other exposure tactics now exist for terrorists to exploit. Lacing body products like sun screen with toxins is one creative way terrorists could disguise a chemical agent's presence and easily distribute it to the general public.

Strong Interest in Using Cyanide
History's use of cyanide as a weapon is well documented. Plots involving cyanide in the past decade suggest its appeal to terrorists. Prior to the London Olympic games, a website linked to a terrorist group listed plans to lace skin lotion with cyanide.

One particular detail not often addressed that makes cyanide a potentially effective weapon is it would require the administration of antidote immediately. In the event of a large-scale attack, it is unlikely any healthcare facility would have an ample stock of antidote kits.

Why Sun Screen?
Sun screen, like lotion, would speed absorption of cyanide by opening the pores in the skin. It can also be distributed in mass quantity at simultaneous public gatherings with little chance of detection. People are generally not skeptical of tottles or promotional packets of sun screen handed out at public events.

Additional Scenarios for Disguising Cyanide
Release of hydrogen cyanide gas or contamination with cyanide salts
- Leak through building ventilation systems
- Use fog machines in theaters
- Vaporize through outdoor water misters or misting air fresheners
- Aerosolize in insect repellant
- Blend with hygiene, cosmetic, or medical supplies
- Mix in with the products of a sugar, salt, or beverage company
- Saturate ink used by a major newspaper
- Salt popcorn in movie theaters

3:10 P.M.

"My knee looks horrible!" exclaimed Stacey as she described the horrific red swelling on both sides of her kneecap. "When I peel back the bandage, I can see red welts everywhere that stun gun jabbed me. And it's all puffy around my knee!"

Will heard her wince as she told him about pressing her fingertip around the burn marks. He pulled his knees up to his chest, his heels holding his legs in place against the front of the chair he was sitting on in the corner of the CIA substation's break room. He was at last back "home" at his new living quarters after the long day of red teaming. A phone receiver was pinned between his shoulder and ear as he wrapped his arms around his shins, effectively contorting his body into a tornado posture atop the chair seat. It wasn't entirely a comfortable position, but somehow it helped Will shelter himself against comments of her hurt, a hurt that he tried not to remind himself was caused in part because she had been with him. "Do they still burn?" He hadn't wanted to ask, but knew he owed her this much, the opportunity to vent her frustration in hopes that she'd free herself of any lasting resentment toward him.

Stacey was one of only four people outside the CIA who knew of Will's involvement with the Analytic Red Cell. She was both extremely good-looking and incredibly bright. If her long athletic legs weren't enough to keep Will's mind busy, her sharp wit and cunning retorts made it impossible for Will to concentrate on just what he saw with his eyes. He figured it wouldn't take long for her to realize that last night had not simply been a random attack. It worried him that his affiliation with the CIA might make it too hazardous for her to be involved with him. Though some girls seemed to go for a little danger, Stacey had liked him before she knew of any government involvement.

"They still sting. And they make my knees look all blotchy. You're not going to want to look at my legs anymore."

The gasp that left Will's throat after this comment was not so much out of laughter that he could possibly not be attracted to those legs, but relief. An obvious flirt meant that she had not held the attack against him. "I'd love to come and see them now, but I don't think they'd let me leave."

"I figured your mom wouldn't allow you out after what we survived last night," Stacey replied.

"Actually wasn't referring to my mom."

"Your dad started in on you too?"

"Wrong again. I've been placed on an even higher level of security than that."

"No way! Mr. Tenepior's got you?" Stacey had been quick to correctly guess.

Will wasn't surprised about her answer. She had been the one person he could talk to about how deep his involvement with Top Secret CIA operations not even a year ago had been. Though he never truly filled her in on the Red Cell's inner workings, he knew she fully understood why Will had become entangled in national security affairs in the first place. He was also certain she didn't know he still played his role with Homeland Security.

"How'd he get involved?" she asked.

"Let's just say that a stun gun was nothing compared to almost getting my house blown up last night."

"Will! Something else happened? Is everyone O.K.? What's going on?"

The concern in her voice rattled Will a little. He didn't know if she was worried for his sake or chewing him out. Knowing it was better to be straight-forward with her, he explained how the attacks didn't seem random. The dead air he received from her side of the phone was a clear message that she was unnerved; he figured it had as much to do with the cause of last night as it did her not knowing.

He began what he meant to be an apology by saying, "I never stopped working with the Red Cell. Agent Tenepior and I have been bouncing ideas off of each other ever since I stopped Es Sayid's terrorist cell. We talk a couple of times a week from my computer. I wasn't allowed to tell anyone."

Will exhaled, hoping the explanation was enough. He could hear some muffled huffs and her rustling the phone, but she didn't answer. He continued, though it came out more like rambling. "Tenepior thought it best that you not know either. I wanted to tell you. My parents didn't even know…until last night. Now we're stuck here at the substation since there's someone new after me…the same person behind your burn marks."

Silence.

"Stacey, I'm sorry. I didn't know that anyone was after me now. I thought all that ended last year. No one should have known I was involved. Then, just this morning, an operative discovered an internet video that showed one of the terrorists I helped catch screaming out my name. This new guy had to have found out about me from it."

Will waited to hear a response. She still wasn't talking. He thought they had been through enough together that hiding the secret of his operative status from her wouldn't be too big of a deal. After all, it was the way of the service. He was sure they could get through this. But then again, he considered, she hadn't been personally attacked the first go-around. Maybe it was all too close for her. Maybe this had made it real.

"Stacey?" He strained his ears. He thought he could possibly tell something by the way she was breathing, but he couldn't even hear her exhale. He didn't want to hear any sobbing or even sniffles, though even those would seem more bearable than absolute silence. "Stacey, we made it through last night. We can handle this. Don't let this guy hurt us any more than he already has."

And promptly upon saying this, he finally heard the first sounds from her in several minutes. Her cell phone beeped twice as if she had accidently pressed a couple of wrong buttons before a final click and dial-tone signaled their conversation had ended.

3:35 P.M.

Will immediately tried redialing Stacey's number. No answer. He couldn't believe that she'd just hung up on him. Keeping secrets from the person you are closest to is a dangerous game to play, but he still believed their only other argument had been worse. Saving Wrigley Field last year from a terrorist bomber had taught him how much she disliked being deceived. As he considered it that way, this didn't seem all that different. To deceive, something has to be kept from someone. At least last time he'd been able to hear her reasoning as she screamed back at him. This had so eerily been different.

He stood and turned to face the corner wall. Leaning forward, he rested his forehead against it. Forced to stare at the floor, he tried to think it through. After all, figuring things out was his thing; seeing through situations had saved his life before. Saving his relationship was just as important.

The passive gray floor soaked up his thoughts and nerves, melting eye-catching distractions and stressful tensions into a phlegmatic blah. The tiny break room had been avoided by most office personnel since his family had unexpectedly "moved in," giving them full access to the only resemblance of homelike living quarters in the substation. The absence of the usual break-time traffic made the room quiet and lonely.

A fat leaf on an overhanging branch of the potted plant in the corner swayed with his breaths, wavering up and down like his give-and-take thoughts. Stacey had to understand it was his duty to lend his help when he could. Shouldn't trying to do good be worth something? Her reaction hadn't backed this. It wasn't exactly his fault for making this new enemy. He didn't even know the real reason he was being pursued. And her mood hadn't been so terrible when they first began talking. In fact, hadn't she teased him in her flirting way?

His gut kept saying there was something more to this. He knew Stacey. She had completely accepted his role with the CIA last school year. She was a fierce competitor in sports, already making the varsity volleyball squad in her freshman year, so it wasn't like her to get so rattled when the stakes were high. He dialed again.

Nothing.

He dropped his arm to his side and banged his head lightly against the wall, suddenly exhausted. A shutter of panic reverberated down his spine as he recalled the gorgeous smile he often pictured when they were apart— just like it had been the night before. She had cocked her head sideways and smiled at him while they enjoyed ice cream. His lips had ever-so-softly brushed against her hair as he whispered in her ear, breathing in the faint fresh scent of shampoo still lingering even after a full day's activity. Her hand had reached for his. Sliding over his knuckles, her fingers had squeezed her reply. The touch from her fingertips had been thoroughly cooled by the ice cream dish, but he hadn't resisted the embrace, welcoming any sensation of hers.

He continued to dreamily replay his evening with Stacey until he was startled about thirty minutes later by a knock on the glass door. Joe looked at Will and wagged his finger in the air. Most likely, Tenepior had sent Joe to fetch him.

Slumping down the hallway and through the main operations hall to Tenepior's office, he wondered if his operative friend had ever tried to successfully hold a personal relationship of his own with the clandestine lifestyle he had to maintain. Will didn't even know if he was married. Actually, he couldn't think of anything he truly knew about Agent Tenepior's life other than the password "5663" he idiotically liked to reuse. Yet he was sure Tenepior could itemize several hundred details from the life of Will Conlan. It had never been an even share of information. The man definitely guarded his secrets.

As Will came to the office door and peered through the crest-etched glass front, he noticed his parents and a large group of agents crowded around the long table. Agent Tenepior's weight was on his knuckles as he leaned over the table, head hanging to his chest. As Will entered, most everyone turned to face him. His dad's hands firmly gripped the outside of his mother's shoulders. She wouldn't look up at him. Her gaze bore into the rectangular card at the center of the table.

Will instantly knew what the card was. He had been to enough ballgames to recognize the sharp corners and perforated edge of a ticket stub from a distance even if he couldn't yet see the matchup scheduled. As he edged closer he could clearly make out the words "Nebraska" and "Northwestern" typed at the center. A blue-lettered Ticketmaster background slanted sideways across the rectangular length. With realization, his hand involuntarily slapped at the white letters printed across the front of his red Cornhusker t-shirt. "No way! A Husker ticket? And against the Wildcats?" He could barely mask his enthusiasm. "My two favorite college teams. That game's in Lincoln this year. I'd die to go to Memorial Stadium to see it."

His mother yelped at the comment and Agent Tenepior looked up sharply through a raised eyebrow once at Will's mother and then directly at Will. When he spoke, he was direct. "Will, that's sort of the problem."

It was Will's turn to glance back at him; his look, though, carried confusion rather than insight. "The ticket's for me, right? You got me a ticket to a game I'd love to see and now you are telling me there's a problem?"

"We didn't get you the ticket. Your parents were charged for the ticket on their credit card, but they didn't get it for you either." As with any heart-breaking news, Tenepior's speech was matter-of-fact. Emotion was not part of his identity or his job. Inquisitiveness was. "When was the last time you spoke to Miss Chloupek?"

Guarded, Will replied, "About an hour ago. She isn't answering her cell. Why?"

Agent Tenepior handed Will a slip of paper that to this point he had held pinned between two fingers. Unfolding several bends in the paper, he realized the ticket must have been wrapped up within this sheet. The note was relatively short and had been printed from a computer. Addressed to Will, it stated, "If you ever want to see her again, you'll attend the game alone." If the words had not been threatening enough, a pixelated color picture of Stacey clearly bound and gagged had been printed below the words, leaving no doubt as to the nature of the message.

Firmly speaking as Will's face contorted with horror, Agent Tenepior clarified what he knew the truth of the situation to be, "We have sufficient reason to believe she's been taken by the same suspect who's been stalking you."

Will didn't have the opportunity to feel disbelief. That stage of grief was a luxury impermissible in the lives of Red Teamers. He knew there were no impossibilities. Each Red Cell participant lived by the mantra "Our ideas of today are our tomorrow's reality." Certainly no utterance of nonsense had ever left the lips of Agent Tenepior. The instant strain in Will's stomach confirmed this was all too true. His gut had recognized something was off about his conversation with Stacey, a sure sign he had become used to following.

He had known it all along.

And one more certainty struck him as surely as the reality of the ticket—he had heard her being kidnapped over the phone.

4:21 P.M.

"I heard her," Will stammered.

"What was that?" asked Agent Tenepior.

Ignoring the question and continuing his own explanation, Will spoke almost inaudibly through his breath, "I thought she simply wasn't replying, that she was just mad and wanted me to know it. That man took her. And I didn't realize it."

At his defeated tone, his mother grabbed hold of him and wrapped her arms all the way around his back. "You didn't know," she spoke. "It isn't your fault." Her hand was on the back of his head now, patting it down with her palm as she had when he was a child.

He was completely leaning into his mother, his arms hung loose at his sides. "It was happening as I talked. I could have gotten her help."

Cutting in, Agent Tenepior seemed determined to stop Will's sniveling and prevent him from diminishing into a pool of self-pity. "The ticket," he demanded. "Will, time wasted emotionally won't save Stacey. Look at the ticket!"

Will blinked out the blurriness and focused on the stub as he pulled away from his mother. The game, as he already knew, was next week in Lincoln, Nebraska. The ticket seemed authentic, but it still didn't explain the game. "Why? Why the game?" And the more he measured this, it occurred to him, "What game is *he* playing?"

"Exactly!" retorted Agent Tenepior. "Why in the world would you be invited to a football game? And why would it take you being there one week from now to see Stacey?"

All eyes in the room were on him, pleading if not begging. Will knew they all expected Agent Tenepior to have the answer and explain it all back to them. But Will understood that even the words he had chosen were packed with meaning whether or not anyone else in the room would pick up on his subtleties. What hadn't been uttered was the word "save." There had been no indication from the note that Will's attendance would result in the safety or release of his girlfriend.

"How'd he know?" The question was a simple one, but it shook Will the most. This time all eyes moved to Will, but their looks were clouding with misunderstanding. Will and Agent Tenepior knew the routine in their brainstorming. Two steps ahead in their thinking moved their exchanges in giant leaps like solving math equations without showing one's work. Any listeners would surely be confused, not in the conversation's direction, but in its pathway.

"It seems to me that our man knows way more about you than should even be possible. This game has matched your favorite two teams head-to-head. There has to be a reason he picked *that* game. There are no coincidences in his line of work."

"Do you think there's a plot to attack Memorial Stadium? Maybe getting me there would be like trying to kill two birds with one stone?" Will knew it was unwise to suggest the possible danger he'd be in with using such a blatant word as "kill" in front of his mother, but she was involved now and this just wasn't the time to hold any ideas back. Suppressing any thoughts could mean missing important details. He was sure this was one time where his mom wouldn't want anything left to chance.

"Definitely possible. My best hunch would be that he's just trying to get to you. He most likely wants another crack at you and wouldn't have the opportunity with you locked up inside this secure facility. You're harder to protect out there." Agent Tenepior's hand had risen, jutting his finger at the door as he spoke.

Clearly understanding the implication behind Agent Tenepior's words, Will's father explained the foreboding repercussions in his own way. "Can't track the animal that refuses to leave the safety of his den."

In one simple phrase his father had turned the whole situation into a hunt. He didn't have to explain who the prey was.

Though Will's head was still turned to the door after following Agent Tenepior's pointing finger, his mind was far away, already trailing through the University's large campus with the Sea of Red, swarms of eager fans decked out in Husker clothing. Each and every face could be the assailant. Any single person he rubbed shoulders with might strike at point blank range. He could picture it being done almost stealthily with no one even noticing as he crumpled to the cement walkway, a lethal blow received as the crowd panned out in a circle around his body, the attacker engulfed among the onlookers.

"My guess is that Warren is right on. The game may not have anything to do with it, but the stadium itself may be the larger factor," stated Agent Tenepior. "It does allow our kidnapper to blend into a massive crowd, making it virtually impossible to see his assault coming."

"You don't actually expect our son to go through with this?" questioned his mother.

And his father spoke up in turn, "Can't just send a kid to catch a terrorist. No one brings just *one* pail to fight a range fire."

The frustration was clear in their voices. His mother stood rigid, her arms unfurling like wings in front of her with palms up. With an exasperated huff, she showed the universal look of "You've got to be kidding me!"

Though he knew his father was simply looking out for him, Will was frustrated by his father's lack of faith, when, many times before, he had indeed proven himself. Throwing it back at his dad in his own language, he tried reasoning, "Dad, how many times in baseball have you told me that I'm not going to make the play if I'm out of position?"

His father was adamant this time. He shot back so quickly that Will had barely quit speaking. "You don't step to the plate without a bat!" His acidic sarcasm singed the air with each stinging word. Warren stood and strode over to a display case, his hands on his hips and his back turned to the table. It was more than clear he thought Will would save himself a lot of trouble if he just used his head. His angry exhale could be heard across the room.

Knowing he wasn't about to win a battle of words when his dad had grown up on a ranch in Nebraska where talking this way was normal coffee shop chatter, he tried to be as direct with his reasoning as he could, "Hey, it's my call. That note was only addressed to one person." Ever focused on the end goal, he continued, "This is Stacey we're talking about. She's worth any amount of trouble. If that's the only way to get her back, I'm going."

4:42 P.M.

"Joe, get our contacts at Jeppesen on the phone to start arranging the logistics for a chartered flight to Lincoln, Nebraska. Make sure they also provide secure ground transportation when we arrive." Tenepior's instructions were brief and clear. As if he had downloaded blueprints of tactical schematics into his brain, the chief seemed to know exactly how to coordinate each step of the unforeseen mission without second thought.

He ordered another agent, whom he also called "Joe," to arrange an extrication strike force in the event of terrorist capture or Stacey's rescue.

"Joe, I'll also need to contact the University's Chancellor. I'll want to speak to him immediately," he said, motioning to yet another agent wearing a headset who sat at the conference table to his left.

Never taking his eyes from his laptop, "It's Douglas Boyd," said Joe almost instantly, displaying why he was a member of agent Tenepior's team. "I have him on hold for you now."

Not the slightest bit of surprise about the quick response passed over Agent Tenepior's face. He was as calm and collected as ever. He was in his element and must have expected the information to be right at his fingertips. This was the CIA. These guys knew what they were doing.

Grinning, it occurred to Will that Agent Tenepior had just called three different agents "Joe." He wasn't sure if Tenepior was too busy to learn their names or if it was merely standard procedure to not use operatives' real identities around outsiders like his parents. In either case, it was the first amusement he had encountered in many hours.

Will sat down next to his parents on one side of the table and decided to grab a laptop so he could forward his report to his English teacher now that he wouldn't be making it to class this week. It seemed a pointless gesture, but there was no way to explain to his English teacher that a terrorist had ruined his first report. Though it would have been original, Will was sure his teacher had heard his share of "the dog ate it" excuses. Getting at least this much off his mind would help him concentrate on what was ahead of him with the mission. He leaned back in his chair, trying to relax now that at least one grade was repaired, and watched the action of the task room unfold.

Tenepior was at his desk speaking on his phone. Agents came and left his office in such a steady flow that the door never fully closed. Other phones began to buzz, and the interactive whiteboard flicked to life. All the planning and preparation was impressive. Hundreds of angles were already being considered. Opportunities were being assessed. In contrast, Will had always thought that if he wasn't tailgating, going to a game usually didn't mean much more than picking out the right clothes to wear.

Agent Tenepior hung up his phone and walked to the interactive whiteboard. In front of him were images of the University of Nebraska-Lincoln. He manipulated the screen until he had the campus map zoomed in. Naturally picking up the red pen tool from the tray, he began to scrutinize Memorial Stadium's location.

Though Will doubted if Agent Tenepior had ever stepped foot in Lincoln, he marveled at the man's ability to strategically dissect the campus layout into a battlefield. He marked up the screen, noting natural cover for agents, the stadium's choke points in the event of a pursuit, and spots that posed restrictions to surveillance. Still in awe about how the map had just magically appeared on the screen without a direct requisition from Agent Tenepior, Will smiled knowing that "Joe" had obviously done it for him.

"It's all pretty impressive, isn't it?" questioned his mother leaning into his shoulder. Will apparently hadn't been the only one marveling at it all.

"That's why I'm so sure I'll be fine at the game. Look, they've got the entire stadium guarded," he said, waving his arm at the screen. "They'll have eyes on me the whole time."

"Will, just like your father said, things can go wrong." Then after a brief hesitation, she continued, "The only thing that gives me any real comfort is knowing that man is on our side." Her eyes bore into Agent Tenepior's back as she spoke.

Her admiration was not singular. Will sensed that every operative here was not merely following the chain of command as he ordered them about the room. Each would have complied with Tenepior's orders simply out of earned trust and respect. The fact that he could beat them all to a bloody pulp, a fact that Will had personally witnessed, probably didn't hurt either.

"And you haven't even seen him *fight*!" He had meant for the thought to stay in his head, but it escaped his mouth before he could think better of it. His parents hadn't known of his own kidnapping or Agent Tenepior's fistfight against the knife-wielding Es Sayid less than a year earlier. His opponent could have had a samurai sword and it wouldn't have mattered. Tenepior's hands were much more dangerous.

"So, you've seen him fight?" Will's father replied, sizing Tenepior up.

"Well, I have had a terrorist after me before," Will said as innocently as he could muster, trying to be truthful without giving too much away.

His mother saved him from the explanation. She seemed to have taken the comment in a different direction. "Hope Stacey is all right," she said almost to herself. "Joe," she turned to face the agent directly across the table from her, "What do we know of Jon and Nicole Chloupek? Are they safe?"

Though the reply could have come from any agent, the one she had asked spoke up, "They're rattled, but they are in a patrol car on their way here at this very moment."

Agent Tenepior spoke out to Will's parents from the front of the room, "You are going to need to play an instrumental role in helping the Chloupeks cope with the kidnapping of their daughter." Placing the pen tool in its tray, he began walking to their side of the table and continued to talk as he walked, taking advantage of every second at his disposal. "They will surely find comfort in having you here to help them through this."

He sat down on the edge of the table in front of their chairs and rested his hands in his lap. Even this movement appeared to be a tactical choice; he occupied the higher ground, forcing them to stare up at him instead of fully coming down to their level. Will knew from the classroom that his posture might appear conversational, but their talk would be controlled by the information *he* wanted to explain. It was then that Tenepior paused his speaking for the first time. With one hand, he unbuttoned the cuff of his dress shirt and began rolling it to his forearm.

"You have to understand the situation we are in with you here in this room. The normal public does not see this. The less anyone knows, the safer it is for everyone. You have to understand how important that is. I have allowed this privilege out of circumstance and respect for Will. His world, our world, has become part of your own. But it won't for the Chloupeks."

He paused to let the point sink in. The puzzled look on Katherine's face must have given Agent Tenepior the signals he needed. Will knew his mother had a thing against not completely being truthful, and it was apparent to him that she wanted nothing to do with what she was being instructed to do.

Agent Tenepior continued to explain the situation. "Jon and Nicole won't know where they really are. We have arranged for a room down the hall near the rear entrance to serve as a waiting room. They'll remain there while we treat the situation as a normal kidnapping case. We've ordered an Amber Alert and an investigative search. They are to believe this is a kidnapping involving the same suspect who tried attacking the kids the night before. That much is true, but otherwise they will be left completely in the dark as to our primary mission in Lincoln."

"But that's not right! It's not fair to them! They have a right to know what's happened to their daughter!" Will's mother raised her voice as if she were about to lose her control.

Agent Tenepior's gruff voice showed signs of losing his patience. "It may come as a shock to them, even after what they've been through this afternoon, to learn that their daughter's boyfriend has ties to the intelligence world and that she probably wouldn't be included in such a dilemma if it weren't for her relationship with *him*."

His glance at Will was quick but unmistakably regretful. Will couldn't look back at him. Exhaling a huff, Agent Tenepior's next words were softer. "This is not your fault, Will, and I did not mean for it to sound as such." He turned his gaze back to Will's parents. "But you know how the truth will look."

They sat silently, obviously digesting his viewpoint. Will's father swallowed in response. Will guessed it would be an awfully hard truth to explain, one that might destroy the relationship between the two families.

So Agent Tenepior continued by conveying his instructions. "You two will be in the room when they arrive. Not Will. They are to believe he's been kidnapped, too."

"You can't expect us to lie! We won't sit here and act like we share the same tragedy, faking our emotions to mask the truth," Will's mother cut in. "We'll be mocking them. It's outrageous!"

"Outrageous? OK, you be in charge of telling them the best chance of getting their daughter home safely relies on a fifteen-year-old boy!"

Stung, Will slumped down in his chair even further.

Once again, Agent Tenepior backtracked. "No offense, Will. I have confidence you'll succeed, but you have to understand how this all would look. It is for the best."

Will could see the defeat in his parents' eyes—his father's drooped from worry and his mother's darted about with helplessness. The Conlans had gone to battle for what they believed and lost. Clearly, their core principles had been a cause they hadn't realized they would forfeit. This was new ground they were not accustomed to. Tactical situations were a part of Agent Tenepior's "lose and you die" world. Not theirs. It had never been a fair match.

Agreeing to the terrorist's demands wasn't a fair fight either. And Will knew it. He couldn't help but share his parents' feelings. Their argument had shattered his confidence and he was no longer sure he could do this. Going to the stadium alone would put his life in danger. The only people in the world who even remotely would give him a chance to survive were sitting before him. And even Agent Tenepior had revealed his doubt.

Rubbing his sore neck, Will continued to bend over in his chair. Everything had gotten so messed up. His grades were ruined, his girlfriend taken from him, his identity spread throughout radical communities, and he had been attacked twice. This terrorist had destroyed his life in less than two days. Only by luck had he so far survived.

Why would he expect this time to be different? Was it even possible to rescue his girlfriend, halt a possible terrorist attack, and end up making it out alive? He was only a kid—a kid who so far was not winning this battle. And no matter how hard these intelligence officers tried to neutralize the risks, it was pretty obvious he would be walking straight into a trap.

October 23, Lincoln, Nebraska

6:00 P.M.

Will's flight to Lincoln ended way too quickly. The Jeppesen company had chartered a Boeing Business Jet lined with tan leather couches on both sides and a huge 52-inch LED screen wall-mounted chest high on the wooden partition at the end. He had found a game-loaded Xbox 360 under its cabinet and had spent the majority of his short journey sprawled on cushions with an ice cold Coca-Cola and game controller. Shaky hands that he couldn't seem to keep still unfortunately caused him to lose every game and spill some of the pop on his shirt. As a result, he changed and spent the rest of the flight lying on the nine-pillowed bed in the master suite and flipping through apps on the new smartphone Agent Tenepior had acquired for him. He soaked up as much of the peaceful luxury while he could since the mission looming ahead would be full of distress.

Other than the two military pilots assigned to the flight, Will was alone. Though the consensus of Tenepior's advisors was that Will was the target and Stacey just bait, they did not want to risk her life by not following the note's directive for Will to come alone. The Special Forces extrication team would come undercover on a commercial flight to cloak their identities, but their weapons and surveillance gear were cargo on the Boeing aircraft.

Other agents and countermeasures had been put in place throughout the stadium when the decision to send Will to the game had first been made. The agents became t-shirt vendors, ushers, and maintenance crew workers that covertly scanned the grounds and kept watchful eyes out for anything suspicious.

Upon landing, as a precaution, the Boeing taxied to a private hanger in order for Will to unload and avoid the airport terminal. Though the terminal would have been one of the most secure of his destinations, passing alone through the crowds of people freely walking through its corridors had been deemed an avoidable concern.

Will had been instructed to find a cab, specifically Taxi #63, where another agent would be his driver. As it ended up, he didn't even have to look for it. Stepping to the curb, the cab pulled to a stop in front of him. His guess was that a phone call placed by his pilots coordinated this as soon as he walked from the hanger. He probably should have at least acted like he was waving it down in case he was being watched, but that opportunity was lost as he handed over his suitcase to the driver and stepped into the back seat.

Their short, five-mile drive from the airport to the Cornhusker Hotel took him right past the western facade of Memorial Stadium. He stared out the driver's side rear window waiting for the stadium to crest over the elevated expressway as they drove toward downtown. The sheer size of its vertical cement walls broke the horizon to his left and filled the window's entire view, completely taking his breath away. Its towering, smooth tan front reminded him of a colossal sand castle—two parallel keeps at its center stood above, chiseled giant red N's at their tops. Paneled windows, portcullises in pattern, rose above each entry gate, the middle three arching four stories high between the towers. On each end, domed entrances engraved with philosophical quotes stood as sentries over both end zone gates, as they proclaimed their proud reminder of Husker Power. The stadium was a magnificent curving fortress crowning the landscape.

Slumping down in his seat after passing the stadium, Will couldn't wait until he could set foot through its gates. It had been a couple of years since his dad had taken him to a game on one of his visits home to the family-owned ranch, but he could still remember its stunning atmosphere. He thought it could quite possibly be one of the coolest spots on Earth.

He was having a hard time imagining the horror awaiting him in such a majestic place. Was his death meant to be caught on national TV, or was the plot bigger than that? He couldn't help but wonder what type of twisted individual would want to bring death and destruction to such a cherished sports venue, a place where people come to cheer, hope, and enjoy life. Thinking back to saving Wrigley Field, he suddenly realized why Memorial Stadium was too hard to resist. It was more than just a building to the people of Nebraska. To these football faithful, it was their heart and soul. And it was special to Will as well. This sick-minded terrorist was making it clear that he wanted to inflict pain, suffering, and fear, not just for fans, but specifically to demoralize Will even further.

Will's gut told him his speculations were right. This terrorist had been tormenting him all week. One painful hurt after another had been inflicted against things Will valued; his girlfriend, home, grades, and even his stomach had been terrorized. A nervous twitch pulsed in Will's neck as he realized he could also inadvertently be the cause of innocent people getting hurt at the next day's game.

The "We're here," snapped his attention from his thoughts as he looked out the window and found himself parked next to the front doors of the Cornhusker Hotel. From his first glance inside as he opened the door, it looked as if his life of luxury would continue through the weekend. The shiny tiled floor led up to a curving wood grand staircase, a red carpet flowing down its steps. The ceiling rose above the mezzanine on the floor above, its open expanse adding to the hotel's luxurious feel. A brass chandelier lighted the varnished wooden interior and murals of Eden painted within the brick walls. It was quite the place! Will guessed it had often attracted the elite.

A clerk at the front counter passed him an electronic key for his room and advised him to take the elevator to floor seven. A horseshoe-shaped hallway led to room 746, a corner room next to a stairwell marked "Emergency Use Only." He decided the Agency had arranged for this as an easy way out if he got in trouble.

The electronic lock clicked green as he slid his card through. He opened the door and tugged his suitcase behind him. He pushed it to the bottom of the alcove opposite the bathroom and let the door close behind him. A TV and a table stood to the right side of the room in front of him. The foot of the bed stuck out to the left from behind the bathroom wall. He walked past the bathroom and toward the center of the room, noticing the crisp bedspread had been already turned down, ready for its nightly company.

Bending to smooth his hands over the fold, a sudden jerk around his head pulled him backward, a thick cloth clasped over his mouth. Sharp vapors bore into his nostrils. His knees went weak as his ankles began to buckle even before he could squirm. The only thing holding him upright was the arm wrapped around his shoulder locking a hand across his mouth. He tried extending a lifeless arm to pull the hand down with his fingers, but they quickly lost grip and slipped away. His head began to swim with a fuzzy, droopy feeling. He found his neck was unable to hold it up any longer. His last fleeting feeling was being lowered onto the bed, his head thudding against the silky feel of the turned sheets.

8:55 A.M.

His first blink was a strain. Slowly stretching back a watery blur, Will's eyelids allowed a sparkling kaleidoscope to seep in. The darkness retreated with the brief stabs of stinging brightness. Florescent lighting from high above blanketed wooden crates around him. The pull of sleep felt so very heavy. His neck was refusing to work right. Each blink brought more clues: the only natural lighting came from a single window; a lone ladder leaned against a wall below it. It could be a basement, or maybe a storage facility in some factory. He felt so very tired. His eyes wouldn't stay open.

Muffled talking awoke his lids once again. He tried to shake the dull thudding from his head. A shadow told him there was someone near him now. A desk light illuminated scattered papers and a laptop. A man was just off to his left. Squeaking? Did he hear squeaking? Arms were pinned behind his back. Rope. He was tied to a chair. He could hear agitated talking, possibly on a phone as it was one-sided. English. Pins were pricking his toes. His bound feet were asleep. His face flushed with heat, baking the dried spit crusted at the corner of his lips.

Stadium.

He heard someone say "stadium."

Something was tugging him from behind. Talking had stopped. He could lift his head. The man was gone but the computer screen still gleamed. Had the man just vanished or had he fallen back to sleep?

"Will!"

The word hit him solidly. It had come from behind. He snapped his head backward.

"You've got to wake up, Will. Help me. He's left. I think I can get my hands loose. We've got to get out!"

We've? "Stacey?"

His heart began to beat hard. A Red Bull of pulsing blood revived him from his grogginess. In his delight, he tried to pull his arms up to wrap them around her, but only managed to yank her arms hard against the chair back. They were tied together.

"How? I can't believe you're here!"

"Help me. Can you pull the rope at the back of my wrist with your fingers?" asked Stacey.

Will could hear the hard exertion of her anxious breathing and grunts as she pulled with her hands. He drew backwards with his arms and managed to flick his fingers against her hands, feeling for rope. Using the tip of the longest of his fingers, he pushed down on the top of the loop, budging it slightly as he felt it move against her skin.

"Hurry! He's got some plan to poison everyone at the game. He's been preparing for it all night long as you slept."

"Agent Tenepior thought there might be an attack at the stadium," admitted Will as he strained his finger against the ropes.

"I've about got it past my pinky. Push down more!" she ordered.

The adamancy of Stacey's sharp voice startled some mice held captive in cages behind Will. They began squeaking rapidly and scurrying through the wood shavings in their cages.

"But how can that be right?" thought Will almost immediately. *"He sent me a ticket to the game. Then why was I kidnapped?"* Just as the thought crossed his mind, a side door opened and Stacey quit tugging.

A man walked in, carrying a TV in the clutches of his arms. Will recognized the man almost immediately. The clearest view of him had been at the ice cream parlor, where his venomous eyes had bored into the faces of his group as they ate. Will could see the week of consternation, fueled by hopeful vengeance, was scrunched into lines around his eyes. A yellowing cheek now prominently marked his face. Will hoped the fall down the stairs had hurt.

The man spoke as he set the TV down on a wooden crate, "Will, glad you've decided to join us." Mockingly, he held his hand out for Will to shake as he approached, but Will was obviously inhibited by the rope. A huge rectangular red blister streaked across the man's thumb and backhand. The red leathery welt was charred white around the edges. "Ah, yes. As it is, I guess we've already met." He withdrew his hand, paced a few steps, and pulled both hands back behind his waist as if ready to give a lecture.

"Clever work with the iron, by the way." He drew his arm out from behind him and waved it in the air as he spoke, "Gave me the idea to pay your girlfriend a visit."

At that comment, Will thrashed in his chair, straining his arms and baring his teeth as they gnashed together with anger. He jerked upward, trying to stand. His outburst only worked to yank Stacey backward as she yelped at the sudden tug of her arms.

"You leave her out of this!" Will cried.

Seizing the sleeve of Will's red t-shirt, the man yanked down hard to pull Will back to his seat. So forcible was the tug, Will's sleeve ripped off, tearing at the seam. The hard jerk sent a twinge through Will's neck as his rear end slammed back onto the chair.

"How noble!" The attacker's sarcasm dripped its slime from each consonant. Glancing at the loose fabric in his hand, he turned and stepped a few paces away, stuffing the cloth in his pocket as he strolled. "I should actually thank you for stopping me earlier," he called out over his shoulder, his tone now much lighter. Then lazily leaning his body against a crate and turning back toward Will, "It's given me an even better opportunity to relish the suffering you'll be put through. I'm going to make it so much more *emotionally* painful. Your life will be ripped away in ways you could never imagine—all so I can witness that very moment when you finally realize there's no hope left. You'll be beaten and you'll know it. It's my favorite part. It'll make everything so worth it." He spoke slowly, as if savoring every vengeful word. The rising cheer in his voice heightened the villainous chuckle rumbling from his chest.

The sound made Will shudder. He wondered if all malicious people had some creepy nuance that manifested when the evil was closest. Many nights the reflected glow of Es Sayid's fang-filled grin had caused him to wake in a panic, his subconscious reliving horrible nightmares that really had happened. Will had seen that pleased look just as the terrorist tried strangling him to death. It was probably the effect of crazed insanity. And from his trembling, Will got the worst feeling a new nightmare was taking over.

9:45 A.M.

Will tried to absorb as much as he could. Listening to this man's ranting was one thing, but sorting through every detail might give him the opportunity to find some means of getting out of this horrible mess. He took note of anything his eyes and ears could consume. From the man's skin tone and his Middle Eastern accent, Will decided he was definitely kin to the men he fought against last year.

"So who are you and what do you want with us?" asked Will.

"My name is Azad, and you are going to help me attack a football stadium."

To comfort himself, Will wrapped his pinky around Stacey's. Though it was upsetting that he had gotten her into this, it was comforting to feel her hand in his. He squeezed tighter. If this was to be his last chance to be with her, he was going to hold on to it until the very end.

Azad walked over to the table. He picked up a USB thumb drive from the table and held it up between his fingers. Turning to face Will, he confided, "The plans contained on this drive are not completely mine. The original plans to strike America's beloved sports stadiums belonged to a fellow CLOSER who was hung for what your country calls 'acts of terrorism.' He was my friend, my brother. And you were responsible for his capture and death."

Will figured a "closer" was some freakish Hacker term from all the things Azad had already done over the internet to punish him, so he could see where this was headed. "You are the one who posted the video of his hanging on the internet." He knew. It wasn't a question.

"I see you've had a chance to witness my friend's execution. Did you relish his death?"

The question completely caught Will off guard. He did not think killing a person for any reason was humane. In fact, he was quite repulsed by the verdict the man had received. It had been a just punishment, but that didn't stop Will from feeling the way he did. Killing outside of self-defense, in his opinion, was just plain wrong. "I was only shown the video after you attacked my house. There had to be a reason for you coming after me, and we were looking for answers."

Then figuring he had nothing to lose, Will, with bitterness, continued, "Your friend wanted to kill people. I guess you can say he succeeded at least once."

"Oh, you *are* clever. Though I fail to see how that sharp tongue of yours can cut through that rope around your wrists," Azad retorted.

The comment stung. It was hard to argue against common sense. Calmly searching for another angle, he decided to be direct and just ask for the information he wanted to know. "What is it you have planned for us?"

As if patting Will on the head for participating, the man shook the thumb drive up and down with his hand as he spoke. "Not so clever to figure it out for yourself, though, are you? After our previous encounters, I was expecting more. I would have thought the football ticket was a rather obvious clue." Inserting the devise into the laptop's USB port, he asked, "Rather be told than have to guess?"

Will let his stare be his answer.

"Maybe I overestimated the ability of the world's youngest intelligence operative. If you aren't going to play along, I might as well let you see for yourself. The video I've recorded here was too quickly done to be my best work. What I did last night to the GPS on that new smartphone of yours, on the other hand, was a better fit for my capabilities. Those CIA friends of yours are probably running all over town trying to find you."

Deftly running his thick fingers over the computer's touchpad, the man first opened a video file that showed two mouse cages. From the scattered wooden crates and shallow lighting, Will could see that the video had been recorded in this very warehouse. Two little white mice scurried around in each cage. The camera was zoomed in so that the identity of the man on film could not be seen, but showed enough of his body and arms to easily see he was testing something on these rodents. Will knew what lay ahead for the mice was not going to be pretty.

One gloved hand held a sandwich slice of cheese. Another hand came into view holding a glass jar with a crystalline substance; it looked like a very fine salt. Carefully using a spoon to scoop and dabble a small amount of the powdery material from the canister onto the cheese, a hand opened a hatch at the top of one of the cages and laid the cheese inside.

The mice did not hesitate. They started nibbling corners the second he removed his hand. Will watched as nothing seemed to happen, completely engrossed with anticipation. He already had figured what was going to transpire, but guessed it was also to be *his* fate and couldn't remove his eyes.

At first the mice showed no abnormal behavior. They crept from corner to corner, noses and whiskers wiggling until the time-lapsed film sped up the process. Each of the mice began to shake its head from side to side, obviously disoriented, and started to walk clumsily. They would run into the wire rails of the cage, rear back, and ram into them again. Their tails were no longer being used for balance and slapped about continuously in random directions. One mouse began vomiting as the other keeled over on its side, rapid pants extending its chest with nonstop pumps. Before long, both mice were dead.

The video continued, but this time showed the second cage. The exact same experiment took place with the next two mice but with a much smaller slice of cheese. This time, though, as their behavior became erratic, a new slice of cheese was procured and placed before the mice. The footage showed the cheese being sprinkled with a white, powdery substance from a plastic Ziploc bag. This time as they ate, their behavior returned to normal and it seemed the mice were fine. This clip had been much quicker, ending in just over half a minute.

"Hamid and Mahmoud can thank us for the antidote that saved their lives from cyanide poisoning. They seem to be doing quite well don't they, Stacey?"

Though she had been facing the mouse cage this whole time, she didn't reply, maintaining her silence in quiet disgust. From what he could see of the cages with his head turned, Will guessed Stacey had witnessed the man conduct the actual test that was now being shown to him on the video. The plastic Ziploc bag containing the powdered antidote still lay beside the cage, its deflated top bent over against its weight.

"I don't think George and Barack fared so well," Azad quipped with a smile.

"You gave the ones who recovered Hydroxocobalamin." Will stated it matter-of-factly as if he knew all the ins and outs of bioterrorism.

Unfazed, the terrorist didn't seem surprised at all about Will's root knowledge of the topic. He calmly replied, "I can see why the CIA has been so eager to use you. It's only fitting that such a corrupt organization would use children to do their own dirty work."

Sick of the whole thing, Will shot out, "So you're going to exterminate all the mice in Lincoln. The mayor might give you a medal."

"You could say that. In fact, fans of your favorite team will be the first rodents to go." As if giving an oral report to a class, he clicked another video icon that opened to show two men who wore the green polo shirts of fast food employees. One was shoving paper cups into a dispenser as the other stocked the shelves under the counter with bags of spice mixes and flour.

As if on cue, the clip continued to new surveillance footage of both young men, arms full of similar supply bags, walking into a service entrance of what Will guessed to be Memorial Stadium. Looking closely at the footage to make sure, he noted that one of the employees had poorly shaped teeth, his jaw protruding out with the overbite of a prehistoric caveman. The other was so ordinary in appearance that he would easily blend into a crowd, not even an oversized freckle to help him stand out. He was better built than average, but was not big enough to draw attention.

As they worked, Will tried his best to figure out what restaurant they were working for, but each time they turned toward the camera, a bag of ingredients or a countertop blocked the logo printed on their chest pockets. He knew he'd seen uniforms like them before, but the only restaurant that came to mind that used green as a dominant color was Subway, and he didn't think subs were served at games.

As he strained to mentally capture the details from the video, his attacker continued explaining, "As you can see, we've already managed to smuggle the poison into the stadium. As the game begins, people will enjoy the meal they just purchased, but won't realize it has a special ingredient sprinkled on top. Our 'salt substitute' probably won't be as tasty, but no one will likely live long enough to complain."

Will couldn't help but imagine his I-Search paper. This was *his* idea. The only difference was the size of the target, a big score against 91,000 people.

"What makes you think you won't get caught? You sent the ticket to the substation. The CIA knows your target," Will said impatiently.

"Oh, I wanted them there. I knew they'd come. Can't you see? That's all part of the plan. Call it a fun extra challenge. And besides, it'll even be more gratifying if a few of them die, too."

"So you just used me to get at them?" asked Will.

"Once again, I am unimpressed by the CIA's star pupil," remarked Azad.

Stacey chose this moment to end her silence. "He's got your fingerprints all over those bags of poison. Did it while you were passed out."

"You're going to try to frame me, too?" Will spat with exasperation.

"I think it'll look pretty convincing," Azad remarked.

Stacey spat back, "You're a lunatic! You are trying to hurt us to get back at Will for capturing your friend? He's dead. He won't know about any of this. You can stop it from happening and let us go. He can't get anything out of it now."

"But *I* can. I'm enjoying your pathetic pleading right now. Oh, how I love the suffering!" For effect, he walked over and turned on the TV. "I don't want you to miss any of this—the game's about to start." He then turned and started to walk toward the door. The voices of announcers trying to speak over the cheering fans began to fill the room.

As if discovering a hidden clue, Will yelled out with insolent spirit, "Your plan will fail because they'll know I was never there!"

From behind, Azad pulled a single rectangular ticket stub out of his back pocket and held it into the air. Will instinctively knew it had been stolen from his own pocket. The entire CIA would be waiting for that barcode to be scanned for proof of Will's arrival at the stadium.

Suddenly the man twisted and reached into another pocket. He pulled out a different ticket and held it long enough for the two of them to see what it was before allowing it to fall freely from his fingertips. "Had one of my own, just in case, but I won't be needing it now." Azad's open fingers stayed dismissively in the air as the unneeded ticket skidded onto the concrete floor with a puff of dust. "Does it pain you that capturing my friend last year hasn't changed anything at all? Crowds of people will still die. It must be tough to finally realize there's nothing you can do to stop it." His smugness goaded his lips into curling upward as he stood there. The nonchalance of his loitering infected the air like bragging.

Azad's pause gave Will time to comprehend the ineffectiveness of all his efforts. They had amounted to nothing. Will had, in essence, only succeeded in making this devastating plan a reality—a reality in which he now appeared to be the cause.

Pausing in his step to watch them closely, the terrorist continued, "A four-hour game is a long time. You'll get to see the cameras pan the crowd as many begin to cough. Then they'll have a hard time standing or even sitting, finding they can no longer breathe. Some will even start vomiting. They won't know what's happening to them, but you will. You helped make it happen. You'll get to experience the death cries of tens of thousands."

Opening his arms wide as if he were ready to greet them with a full embrace, the man cheerily proclaimed, "Then when they're done, it'll be your turn. It is all to be your death penalty. The public will cry for it. As you cringe and writhe in a prison cell feeling the pain of these thousands, maybe then my brother will find his peace. It will give me great pleasure knowing you are feeling the pain he felt in his execution."

11:00 A.M.

At the clump of the door's closure, Stacey again began struggling against the ropes. From the TV, a referee's whistle signaled the start of the game and the football was kicked end-over-end high into the air as red uniformed Husker special teamers stampeded downfield in chase. Bright flickers of the screen's sprinting players illuminated Will's face as Stacey heaved and jerked behind him. Frantic tugging began against her left pinky and Will could feel her urgency. He pulled his arms back and forth as he tried to wiggle the ropes past her finger.

A small Northwestern running back took the ball straight up the middle on the first play. Evading four tacklers and zigzagging his way around the middle linebackers, he galloped thirteen yards.

Stacey's pinky came loose and pulled out from under the first loop. Sharply bending the back of her wrist, she was able to continue the rope's path over finger after finger until her left hand was completely free of the tightest loop.

The fullback took his turn to the right, pulling loose from a weak arm tackle, but lost his legs and wobbled like a roller pin over the backs of two fallen linemen. Second and four with just over forty seconds played, the Wildcats already were one first down away from midfield. Each play intensified Will's panic. They might not escape in time. People were being poisoned with each second of the play clock.

Using the new slack, Stacey pulled up her wrist, the last two wraps of rope reaching underneath Will's fingertips. By sliding his fingers between her wrist and the rope, he managed to loosen a loop enough for her to pull down and slip her hand free from the last bindings.

With a quick release, the quarterback threw a bullet between two defenders who converged from both sides of the slant route, the ball whisking through their diving outstretched fingers and cradling into the arms of the receiver.

With her free hand, Stacey worked at the knot around her other wrist, loosening each line as she looped the end through crossed strands. In less than two minutes working together, Stacey stood freely, pulling herself up from the chair, the rope falling away from her wrist.

Dropping the ball to the red-painted turf behind his back, the receiver raised both triumphant arms to the small square-cornered section of purple-clad screaming Wildcat fans. The underdogs had struck first and scored the first points.

Hearing the scooch of her chair and feeling the pull against his ropes slacken, Will knew she was free. "You are amazing," he muttered with astonishment and relief. He had always thought it, but this was just more proof. She had made slipping away from the rope seem so easy.

Stacey turned to his back and began working on his ropes. "Will, what are we going to do?"

She pulled at the back of his hands, unlacing the knots until he could yank his arms free. The question of what they could do was much harder to unravel. How could they save almost a hundred thousand lives, especially if they'd already purchased tainted food? The only chance they had was to get to the stadium, stop the concessions from making any more food, and find Tenepior.

Jogging a few strides across the floor, Will bent down and grasped the unused Husker ticket. Bringing it to the edge of his lips, he blew against the cardboard surface, an eerie billow of dust contaminating the stale air around him. "We've got to get to the stadium and fast!"

"How do we get out?" asked Stacey.

"The jerk took my new cell phone." Looking over at Stacey, he questioned, knowing the answer before he even asked, "Does he have yours too?"

"I think I dropped it on my bed when he had his hand over my mouth."

Will stood and looked around the room to survey his choices. He cupped a hand around his left wrist and twisted it from side to side, trying to wring some sensation back into his hand. "Since calling's not an option, we could try the door, but it's probably not worth chancing a run-in with any guards."

As an answer, Stacey lifted the rope still gripped in her hands and tugged on both ends, snapping the rope with a twang. "If we do, we can give them a little taste of their own medicine."

She seemed like she meant business and her fierceness gave him pause. "Wait. That's a perfect idea." He let go and ran back to the area with the chairs, his eyes intent on something he had seen there.

The mice had their own medicine. They were proof of the tragedy to come and the cure to save them all. A saving chemical these creatures had digested was coursing through their bloodstreams, fighting hard to mop up the destructive cyanide poison. The antidote was the answer. He'd need to take the Hydroxocobalamin with him to Memorial Stadium. Agent Tenepior's response team would be able to figure out how to use it and get the spectators the help they needed.

Wild chattering came from the two mice as Will approached. As he touched the cool metal wire of the cage, the mice with their matted white fur scurried to bury themselves nose first under wood shavings. They obviously had regained fear for the ways of man. They looked alive enough to Will. That white powder had done the trick.

Reaching over to the gallon-sized antidote bag that sat on the crate next to the cage, Will realized it didn't seem that big. He picked it up by the purple-fastened top to gauge its weight. It couldn't weigh more than a few pounds. He knew there wouldn't be nearly enough. But then again, he thought, maybe it was the proof he needed. The contents of this bag verified the unfolding plot within the stadium. Will knew the CIA had reviewed the evacuation procedures for the stadium in the event that an attack might occur. Medical emergency response teams were going to be in place inside buildings and cloaked within tailgate parties around the stadium. He and Stacey were not alone. Nor were the intended victims in the stands.

Instead of putting the bag into front pockets where ticket takers would easily see it, Will pulled up the back of his t-shirt and wedged two bulges of powder around his shorts' waistband so the bag wouldn't fall out as he walked. They just had to find the right people, Tenepior's men, and they would have their help. No other adults, including stadium security, would believe their story.

"Hurry, Will." Stacey's long legs couldn't keep still; her feet stirred up puffs of dust as she shuffled back and forth.

Tucking the bag more firmly against his back with his palm as he hobbled toward her, Will stopped himself in front of the desk. Taking hold of the laptop and peering at the paused video he'd been shown on the screen, he yanked out the thumb drive and shoved it into his cargo shorts' pocket.

Earlier, as the video revealed the dying mice, he had thought it unwise for his attacker to show them exactly what they were going to do. Being taught how to play Five Card Stud at an early age by his grandmother, he understood advantages were lost by giving away your cards. He had decided between flickering images of staggering mice that if he were able to escape he'd somehow steal that thumb drive. In their rush for freedom, he had almost forgotten his plan.

With one last swipe, he frantically ran his hands through the papers lying on the tabletop. There were notes and order forms, but nothing else seemed really substantial. They had their necessary proof. Now they just needed to get out of this building before they were caught.

11:15 A.M.

"I can tell you've got a plan running through that head of yours," commented Stacey.

She evidently had more faith in her boyfriend than their attacker did, thought Will. "There's no way of knowing what's waiting for us behind that door. Our only other option from what I can tell is the window. Do you think I can hoist you up from the top of that ladder?" he asked.

"Let's use it to stack more of those wooden crates. We can climb to the window from there," replied Stacey.

Will knew her approach would take longer, but it would allow both of them a sturdy platform to stand on together. In answer, he grabbed the bottom edges of a crate and scooted it on top another crate already against the wall. A rough grating noise reverberated from the friction, much like a chair against a hardwood floor. They both shared a quick glance toward each other.

"That was way too loud," Will whispered. More gently this time, he set another crate next to his first to make it double wide. He saw Stacey over his shoulder leaning one of the chairs against the door, its back wedged underneath the handle.

She had done this without direction. Besides her naturally muscle-toned body, reacting innately was one of the traits that made her such a superior athlete. Her anticipation was remarkable and so was she. He wished he could simply watch her and soak her all in. If the fate of tens of thousands didn't solely rest in their hands, he might have contemplated stacking the crates in front of the door instead to keep them trapped here alone together.

Stacey climbed the ladder and helped Will position one square carton after another into a steep, boarded platform until the stacks reached the bottom of the window. The glass itself was secured by two hinges, allowing them to tilt the bottom half outward and thus open their newly made escape route.

Stacey peered her head out the window. "Will, that looks like a long way down."

Will jutted his head through, holding carefully to the sill so he wouldn't fall. Many rows of bricks layered the wall beneath him. "Yeah, that's gotta be at least twenty feet. We could probably make it if there was something to land on."

"It'd take that man charging after us again with his stun gun to get me to jump that."

Will turned his body and leaned sideways against the window casing. He looked around the room to see if there was anything to use. Stacey was already stepping down the ladder.

"So how low to the ground would it have to be for you to jump?"

She stopped on a middle rail and looked back up at him. "I'd guess ten foot's probably the max."

"Then crawl back up here and help me tow the ladder up."

Clearly beyond second guessing him, Stacey joined him on the crates and pulled the top step of the ladder upward. Will lifted until he grasped the bottom step and slid its rails out the window until its metal spreader bar rested on the sill. The rear support legs remained inside the building, helping to pin the ladder to the wall.

"If we can manage to climb down the steps on the outside, that should cut the fall in half," Will said. He then wiggled his body feet first through a gap between steps, sliding across the rungs on his stomach. Using the steps, he climbed downward until he could grab the last rung firmly with his hands. Bracing his soles against the brick wall, he slid his hip off the last step and dug the tips of his shoes into the mortar to take the weight off his arms. As if doing a reverse chin-up, he let his arms extend until his body was dangling from the bottom of the ladder midair. He then let go. Twisting and falling sideways to avoid spraining an ankle, his shoulder and thigh hit the ground. Luckily, the powder-filled bag at his waist didn't pop.

Stacey didn't waste any time and landed on her feet next to him. She mocked, "You weren't very graceful, but your plan still worked."

All around them were brick warehouse buildings and store backs. He hadn't the foggiest notion where they'd been taken. Pointing a pathway to freedom lay two parallel railroad tracks running behind the buildings. It was tempting to follow the endless unblocked path and simply get away, but there were people that needed their help and they needed to find them.

Stacey clutched Will's forearm, her other arm out in front of her pointing to the sky. From above the building tops rose thousands of red balloons floating toward the clouds. The sky was filled with dots of red, white streamers wagging behind each. On former football trips to Nebraska, Will had seen this balloon spectacle almost block out the sun when the Huskers scored their first points of the game.

"Guessing the stadium's that way," Stacey said, still pointing toward the balloons.

By the antique feel of the buildings lining the street they were running down, Will saw they had stumbled into the historic Haymarket of Lincoln. The brick fronts showed off a quaint collection of little merchandise shops, warehouses, restaurants, and even a train depot all styled in the character of their 1800's heritage. Holding on to each other's hands as they sprinted, they dashed onto the bricked street as they made their way around steps when the sidewalk rose to patio level in front of a store entrance.

As they ran, Stacey finally got around to saying what had probably been on her mind since he had shown up drugged and fast asleep. "At first I wanted to blame you for getting me involved in all this," she confessed. "Then he started messing with those mice. It was horrible. They lay there jerking and twitching and I thought they'd never stop. I began hoping he wouldn't find you and kept praying you'd get the CIA to come rescue me."

Her words exposed a fragile vulnerability that belied her running, and Will couldn't find fitting ones to speak in return. Finally, he settled on clarifying, "Actually, I *was* trying to come get you."

The roar of a motorcycle cut off his explanation. Ahead of them, a green-shirted man plopped his body down on the cushioned seat and twisted his wrist to rev the motor's throttle. The chin straps from his helmet dangled loosely at his neck as he lifted the kickstand with the back of his heel.

A plume of billowing gray exhaust from the bike's tailpipe engulfed their running legs as they passed behind, their rubber soles slapping at the road's smooth bricks. From the diagonal parking slot, the biker backed out in a curve across both traffic lanes until he faced the same direction

Will and Stacey were running. Lifting his leg from the road, he steered the bike forward.

Marking their distance between oncoming vehicles, Will pulled Stacey across the street as he looked back over his shoulder and caught sight of the rider's unmistakable overbite protruding above his leather chin strap. As if a snarling dog had snapped its teeth directly at him, Will realized that he had seen that jaw before. The film footage replaying in his mind of this guy stocking shelves within a concession stand sent a shiver of anxiety wafting across his skin.

Firing the engine by throttling up, the man began riding down the street towards them. The pounding of Will's heart increased rapidly as he tugged Stacey past the corner of the first building's edge. He had to think quickly. Was fate providing him with this opportunity to reduce the overwhelming odds against them by one? His run slowed as much from this thought as the effort it took to jog up the street's steep incline. He ducked his head under the hollow tubes of a wind chime that dangled from the overhang of a shop. It was one of many items that decorated the awnings of each storefront. Dodging other hanging items as he ran, he began to squeeze Stacey's hand harder in his panic.

Will knew she sensed his tension. She questioned, "Will, what is it?"

"The guy. The motorcycle. He's one of them." His anxious breaths, impeded by their running up the steep street, cut sentence structure with each gasp. The motorcycle's mufflers bleated loudly as the cyclist turned the corner behind them. Will needed something that would stop this guy, and quick.

A boutique directly ahead was decorated with uniquely designed flower pots hanging at the corners of its awning by wire. The nearest must have been made by an artistic rancher as various types of old barbed wire wove a threaded vine-like pattern around the pot's brim. Releasing himself into the air and yanking it down by its base, Will had grabbed the only immediate thing that he might be able to use to stop the rider.

Whipping her head around, Stacey yelled, "Will, I think he's coming after us!" Will glanced over his shoulder to see the biker angling his path directly toward them.

Palming the orange basin like a shot putter, he would try to angle his toss at the right moment to peg the biker's head and knock him off the bike. He calculated that, if being pelted didn't stop him, at least the barbed wire was going to hurt. It wasn't the first time a victim of his had been inflicted with a bloody wound or two.

Still running but with her head completely turned behind, Stacey screamed, "He's right behind us!" Accelerating against the hill's incline, the motorcycle suddenly gained speed.

Without warning, Will leaped into the air and twisted his body completely around until he was looking directly into the helmeted face of the oncoming motorcyclist. Chucking his improvised weapon with all his might, Will thrust his arm forward. Granules of dark black soil showered out as the pot shot through the air. The centripetal force of his spin pulled his toss off target as the pot whirled through the air. He could see the projectile would miss the rider completely. Will watched, realizing he had bungled his chance.

But as he threw, the biker swerved to avoid the flying object by leaning his bike toward the middle of the street. As the tumbling shell of soil dropped downward past the man's body and engine block, its falling arc angled perfectly into the leaning rear wheel well. Shattered pottery and dirt exploded through the spinning aluminum wheels. Loosened strands of barb wire kinked and caught against the alloyed bars, coils wrapping around the chain sprocket and catching against its rear swingarm. Locking the wheel with a sudden wrenching jerk, the rear end of the motorcycle shot upward, flipping itself over the front, the rider catapulting from his seat. Chunks of fiberglass shattered and sparks shot up as the bike crashed end-over-end. Crunching against the street, the man's body bumpily skidded across the bricks until it slammed into the undercarriage of a parked car, limp tattered legs bent around its tires.

11:30 A.M.

Running from corner to corner, Will and Stacey crossed car-packed streets as blocks passed behind them. Will, never once stopping, had been pulling Stacey's hand the entire way. The longer they ran, the more Will realized that he'd probably made a huge mistake. "We shouldn't have run. We should have stopped long enough to check over that motorcyclist for clues."

Breathing hard from their frantic run, Stacey replied, "Don't you think getting the antidote there is more important? Isn't that why we've been running this whole time?"

"I ran because we'd have never gotten out of there if we'd had to explain ourselves to a bunch of adults. But if there had been a cell phone in his pocket, we could have called Tenepior." It was a rookie mistake not to consider the sheer importance of what he could have communicated. They had actually lost time by running away. Every ball player knows the ball always travels faster than the runner.

"True, but we know what Azad looks like. They don't," countered Stacey.

"So just how are we going to locate these last two terrorists in an entire stadium filled with thousands of people?" Will, still not convinced, asked. "We could run around the whole stadium from vendor to vendor and completely miss them. We don't even know which concessions are involved."

And with that thought, the answer hit him like a brick.

"Was there any particular logo on that biker's shirt?" he asked Stacey as they were now running past the red brick and wooden doors of the campus's distinctive Architecture Hall.

"It all happened so fast. I don't know. His shirt was an ugly shade of asparagus," Stacey replied.

"And tan pants, right?" Will asked as he tried to fill in his own gaps. His memory flipped through the endless order counters of fast food chains he had frequented throughout childhood before deciding there were only a few food options at Memorial Stadium. "I think I know where to look for the other two." Thinking once again of his perfect act of terrorism report, "They're going to lace Runzas with cyanide at one of the concession stands. My guess is that biker was wearing a Runza uniform."

"They have fast food restaurants in the stadium?" Stacey asked.

"Actually, I only remember concession stands. But I'm pretty sure the food vendors that walk up the aisles wear Runza shirts or aprons."

"Then we'll just have to focus on the ones wearing green." She paused to breathe as they ran forward. With a suddenly quicker step, she continued, "We're going to do this. We're going to save these people." She said it so definitively, his confidence was bolstered too.

Channeling his nervous energy, he pumped his hand that still held Stacey's. He had escaped being kidnapped by terrorists, learned the attack plans for the game, and found Stacey. The first parts of the mission had all fallen into place. "Yes, we can still do this!" He practically shouted this as they reached the first gates of South Stadium. These were student gates, structured with white metal dividers to filter the hordes of students into organized lines.

Wrapping his fingers around the cardboard strip in his pocket, Will realized that he didn't have one for Stacey. Holding it out to show her, he found himself ashamed that he hadn't considered this problem before. "Maybe this is better. I wouldn't want you in there with them anyway. Go. Find a phone. Call Tenepior and let him know where you are and tell him to send his security to take you someplace safe, somewhere a long way away from here."

Without letting her reply, he turned to the ticket taker and requested a pen. "Give me your hand," he said to her and wrote Tenepior's ten-digit number he'd memorized a long time ago. "Explain the plan and where he can find me. I'll need his help. And don't tell anyone else or this could all backfire."

She didn't reply. She just took hold of him, her arms around his back, and kissed him. Though she didn't know the whole story behind the self-sacrificing position he had put himself in to come rescue her, she whispered into his ear as she hugged, "Thank you for coming after me." As she leaned back, her eyes were moist and her nose crinkled. Releasing him from her grasp, she looked directly into his eyes and ordered, "And you better make it safely back to me!"

11:40 A.M.

Stepping through the gate, Will was immediately accosted by a burly paramedic. Striding forward from beneath the shadows, the paramedic called out toward him, "Will Conlan?"

Will met his gaze and instantly knew the action had been a telltale verification of his identity. As much as his name confirmed who Will was, it also informed Will that the paramedic was one of Tenepior's men and the uniformed black pants and short-sleeve white polo were just a disguise.

Speaking into a walkie-talkie the undercover agent had just unclipped from his belt, he stated, "This is Gate 24. Little duckling's come home."

Will rolled his eyes. Feeling a little insulted at being referred to as a "little duckling," he wondered if all agents were forced by some weird fraternity of operatives to speak in coded nursery rhymes. It somehow made the agent seem less manly.

"We've had agents posted at each gate watching for you." Cutting right to the chase, he asked, "Where have you been?"

Will took a second calculating exactly what to say when, all of a sudden, he spotted his attacker. Azad had just walked off the bottom of a ramp and was meandering through the throng of people at a concession stand. His unmistakable, calculating eyes flickered from person to person as he jostled through the crowd of people. The ferocity fuming with each look made it clear he was up to no good. Will could see that his shirt was black, and an unmistakable green Runza visor brimmed his head. Will couldn't believe his luck. They couldn't afford to lose him.

Shouting out as he thrust his pointed finger in the man's direction, "That's one of the terrorists!"

"There's more than one?" questioned the undercover agent.

"Two more! They're going to attack the stadium. That's one of them—the guy with the bandaged hand and bruised face!"

The agent wrenched his gaze to the spot. Possibly hearing Will's excited voice, Azad turned to look in their direction and immediately removed his visor and threw it to the ground. As his hat was pulled away, Will could see the orange end of a foam earplug stuffed most peculiarly into his lobe. Ducking low, he took off running.

Still pointing, Will shouted, "The guy running!"

Taking off, the agent gave chase, leaving Will completely unprotected. The man didn't even pause, his orders transparently clear. Apparently, Will must be dispensable—the terrorist was, without reservation, the higher priority.

From the look of the agent's obvious physical nature, Will had little doubt terrorist number two would be knocked off his list. He didn't waste time in starting off to find the third.

Scanning the first concession stand the terrorist had just run past, Will didn't spot anything suspicious, but he was mainly looking for anyone else wearing a Runza uniform. Continuing in a jog through the walking area beneath the stands, he frantically searched for any clue. Thoroughly scanning the entire area underneath South Stadium without finding anything suspicious, he jogged to the end of Gate 3, jumping a couple rails and diving into crowds of roaming fans to avoid the eyes of any prowling ushers. Pushing his way up the cement stairs, he rushed to a concourse exit to check the concessions of West Stadium.

He found himself once again enclosed underneath another stadium section. He spotted his first likely possibility just past where cashiers rented canvas-backed tan stadium chairs. Hoping to keep unseen, he hid his body behind an entry gate wall and looked around it at the concession stand.

Peeking his head out to spy through spaces in the shuffling crowd and lines of customers, he watched as workers behind the counter packaged Runzas and filled sixteen-ounce cups with pop. One looked like he could be the second Runza employee in Azad's video. Will couldn't remember if that terrorist was as stocky as this worker appeared, but it sure looked like it could be the same guy. Turning his back to Will, he shuffled to the back counter and began situating trays of meat-filled dough after pulling them from the heater. Will couldn't see exactly what he was doing as his arms moved over the trays, but it was obvious this worker was giving the food great attention.

Will realized no one was actually making the Runzas here at the concession stand. That confused him a little. What he had initially envisioned was salting the meat with the cyanide after browning it. At least that's what he would have done before Einstein told him that cooking cyanide would deactivate the poison. He had seen the two men stocking the shelves with the poison in the video. So what did they do with it?

During Will's pondering, the worker had moved out the side door of the stand. Though his back was turned, Will could see the worker scanning the crowd as he unrolled a pair of latex gloves from his palms. Walking through the crowd, he headed for the restrooms across from the stand. As he pitched the gloves toward a trash bin, one swiped against his leg leaving a three-fingered grease stain across his tan pants.

Considering the gloves, a momentary panic washed over Will. The cyanide could really be anywhere. It could already be planted in the food or mixed in with the spices. Perhaps it had been diluted in the pop machine. Or could it be in the ketchup dispensers? Frantic, he twitched his eyes around looking for possibilities.

As his searching eyes scanned every option, he caught the concession worker emerging from the restroom. But he was no longer dressed the same. At first Will didn't realize who he was watching. The man's green polo had been replaced with an usher's orange sleeveless vest. Will only noticed who it was because of the grease stain on the left leg of his tan pants. There was no mistaking it. This man had changed his identity. He was up to something and needed a new disguise to do it. Will could only imagine the villainy it would involve.

Pumping his arms like coupling rods on a train's wheels, Will jumped from around the wall and gave chase down the corridor. Hampered by his exhausting run from the Haymarket and having to dodge a wave of sauntering fans, Will was having difficulty catching up to the disguised usher. Frustrated, Will sprinted with all his might, pushing people out of his way as he bumped against them, keeping his eyes focused on the back of the terrorist.

Then, because he was running so blindly, he collided with an enormous man who had stepped into his path and couldn't get out of the way fast enough. He was dressed in a red cowboy Husker hat and a white doctor's robe that partially hid some of his size. Will bounced against his girth backward over a condiment table and then with a thud to the ground next to the gigantic plastic hotdog the man had dropped in the collision. Next to a Fairbury Brand logo, the words *Der Viener Schlinger* were painted across the plastic hotdog bun. A tube ran out the back to a carted air compression tank. It was the giant hotdog flinging machine that spoiled upper deck fans with occasional freebie food during game time.

Still focused on his target, Will raised his eyes over the huge air gun to see his quarry slipping away. Before the over-weight man was able to recover, Will reacted. Without hesitation, he slapped the ground and threw himself to a squatting posture. Grabbing a round pepper shaker from the ground and shoving it down the metal barrel protruding from the hotdog's end, he hoisted the schlinger by its handgrips and pointed it directly at the terrorist as a path just happened to open through the sea of fans. He took aim and pressed the trigger. The thump of air pressure exploding from the barrel sent the cylinder projectile hurling like a missile.

This time, he didn't miss.

With a crack, the plastic container whacked the disguised usher in the back of the head, sending him sprawling to the cement, arms out to his sides. Handing the air gun back to the white-coated man, Will said, "Call for security." Then he ran to the unconscious man.

Like a blood splatter of a violent crime scene, pepper was scattered all over his body and across the cement. The man lay relatively motionless, knocked out from the blow. Will moved quickly to pat down his pockets as he searched for his method of tainting the food. He found no bags of cyanide or even a basting brush. There was absolutely no clue as to how the terrorists were running their scheme.

Screaming people stormed around Will. One of them was an agent. He forced the crowd to step back by spreading his arms, his CIA badge outstretched in his hand. Kneeling down, he grabbed Will's arm to get his attention. "You Will?"

In reply Will shook his head and stated, "He's hiding something. Poison."

The agent didn't waste time as he started patting down the unconscious man's waist line. Will concentrated on his thoughts, ignoring the crowd's muffled grunts and questioning glances. Sitting back on his heel, knee against the ground, he looked back in the direction he had run. The worker had been fiddling with the Runzas in that concession stand. His hands had been sprinkling the golden brown rolls of meat with seasoning.

The answer was clear. The poison had already been planted and the new batch of treachery was about to be sold to unsuspecting fans. Will couldn't let that happen.

Will looked back at the agent who was still busy body searching the unconscious concession worker. The agent appeared engrossed in his examination, as his hands dug into the bottoms of shoes and felt around the elastic of each sock. The thoroughness of the search agitated Will. This was wasted time they couldn't afford. The poison wasn't there—it had already been used on the Runzas. Standing, he pushed his way through the circle of spectators and took off.

12:05 P.M.

Will sprinted halfway back underneath West Stadium to find the right concession stand. The merchants were still busy. One girl was filling a commemorative cup with pop with one arm while digging underneath a counter for a spare package of replacement cups with the other. The workers were organized and efficient, each one completely focused on fulfilling his or her particular duties. It was easy to see how the terrorist would have gotten away with contaminating the food. Even if the workers were suspicious, no one would have had a chance to check up on him. And what would they have seen? A little extra salt sprinkled on top? No one would question it.

A bald man with strong cheekbones and an angular nose had taken over pulling the trays of lightly browned Runzas from the heating racks. He was squatty, but his body was solid. His sharp features gave him the tough look of a seasoned boxer.

Will walked right up, sliding to the corner so he wouldn't seem to be cutting in line. "Excuse me," he called out to the white-aproned bald man.

The worker gave him a glance that clearly read, "What now?"

"It's urgent that I speak to you for a moment."

The man brushed a little sweat from his brow onto a shirt sleeve and leaned over the counter, his weight on an elbow.

Leaning in, Will tried to say to the man without being overheard, "You can't serve those Runzas."

"What do you mean?" the bald man asked in a manner that clearly showed he didn't like to be challenged, lowering his voice an octave when he spoke the word "mean."

Will tried to whisper his next statement into the man's ear, though it tested his nerve to lean in any closer. "They've been poisoned."

"What?" he said with utter skepticism spread across his face. Like a lightning bolt, his hand shot from the counter and grabbed Will by his shirt front, twisting it in his fist until the cloth had become skin-tight around his chest. Pulling Will off his feet and half way over the counter with his curling grasp, he declared, "Now you listen to me, you little punk. I serve quality food here. You don't like my Runzas, you go complain to someone else. Look, I'm the manager here. I serve thousands every game and there's never been a complaint! Satisfied customers come back game after game."

Now Will was scrambling. This exchange wasn't going so well and he could see that this new batch was going to be needed quickly as the prior packaged stock in the warmer was getting reduced in quantity with each customer's purchase. Not caring anymore whether he could control the conversation, his words were spoken with quick randomness. "I'm not complaining. I love Runzas. Wish we had them in Chicago. The worker who heated those spread cyanide on them."

"Bull." The manager said with finality. He let go of Will and slammed open the side door, removing any barriers between them. Charging right up to Will's face he exclaimed, "I made those sandwiches myself so he couldn't have done a thing to them."

The straight consumer lines now curved around the argument, apparently more curious in the developing spectacle than they were in their own hunger. The other employees averted their eyes and went about their work. Their boss was in a confrontation with a customer, but Will doubted they could hear all that was being said since the man was the only one raising his voice. Will still tried to keep his reasoning low in fear of creating mass panic. Not that it looked like the customers, if they could hear what he was saying, believed a word of it anyway.

"I saw him doing something to them."

"Something? You don't even know what you saw."

"I do know that if you serve *that* food, people are going to die."

Will could see that behind the man a couple of the workers found enough time with the halt in customer requests to begin wrapping the new breaded sandwiches in logo printed sheets of wax paper.

"Get out of here before I call for security."

"Go ahead. I want their help. I know what I'm talking about."

"You don't know a thing!" the manager spat.

Will was angry now. He had gone through too much to be stopped now. His hands were shaking, riddled with worry and frustration. And the Runzas were about to be sold. "I know I've seen that guy and his buddies kill lab mice with cyanide."

"That's it!" The manager lunged for Will, but he managed to duck away. "Security!"

"I'd bet a million dollars that guy just started working here," Will countered as he jumped from side to side, trying to stay away from the strong outstretched arms.

"Doesn't matter a thing," the boss replied as he caught the edge of Will's shirt. "I've got you, you little scum bag. Maybe you'd like to tell your little theory to the police. Security!"

Pulling away, his shirt ripping even further down its side, Will jumped forward toward the concession stand. "People are going to die!" Will shrieked at the man with as much definitiveness as he could muster.

As he yelled out, the first of the newly baked sandwiches was served to a customer. Will panicked. It was happening before he could end it. Police officers were charging forward, alerted now to the disturbance. If he didn't do something immediately, people would be poisoned. Any one of those sandwiches could mean death to the person who ate it. Will knew he'd never be able to live with himself if that happened because he didn't try everything to stop it. Arms of officers began to reach for him, ready to tug him to the ground as the bald man stood pointing at him, his stupefied mouth wide open.

Will knew he had one chance. There may be spectators sick already, but he could still save the people who would have eaten these. He yanked the Ziploc bag of the powdery antidote from the back of his shorts clutching its top between his fingers. Just as the first officer's hands reached him, he yanked the purple zipper. Like bailing water from a sinking boat, he flung its contents into the concession stand at the newly heated trays. If the man wouldn't stop from selling them, Will would make it so the man couldn't. A wave of white powder soared through the air and rained down onto the food. Crushed white crystals engulfed the entire counter, scattering granules into cups, shelves, and even the pop machine's spill tray.

Giving in to the solace that weakened his legs, he allowed himself to be pulled to the ground. Heavy knees pressed into his back as he was rolled over, his arms tugged roughly into handcuffs. He looked through the spread fingers of a hand that pressed his head to the concrete.

The bald stand manager had his back turned, but by the tilt of his head, Will knew he was gazing across the powdered mess. One hand rested on his hip. He cupped the other around the back of his neck and restlessly squeezed his fingers as if soothing some unseen perplexity.

A crowd had given the man and police a wide berth, but stood in a semicircle around the action. Every curious or disgusted eye was locked on Will. Many among the bunch scrunched their cheeks and shook their heads. "Get him out of here," yelled one spectator who swatted at the air as others echoed their booing agreement.

Those looks and sounds meant everything to Will. They proved he had done it. He would no longer have to worry about anyone eating more of those Runzas. The CIA could now concentrate on helping those who did. All three terrorists had been found and stopped. He had saved lives and Stacey was rescued.

The pure joy behind it all was simply overwhelming. It had all worked out as it should. Good had defeated evil. And he, a kid, had once again squashed the destructive plans of vicious criminals feared by the free world. Relishing in his success despite the sheer impossibility of it all, he found he couldn't control the delirious chuckles brooding in his chest.

12:15 P.M.

Three security officers grabbed Will by his arms, tugging him to his feet. Gruffly, he was pulled toward a stadium gate where he suspected a police cruiser would be waiting. "You created quite the mess back there, kid," said the one guard, now pulling Will.

"Actually I was cleaning one up." He didn't mean to say it smartly, but it must have been interpreted that way as the officer wrenched his arms upward hard. So much for thinking his age would gain him leniency.

Will hadn't really considered the way it all must have looked. Some kid picks a fight with a food vendor and wrecks his whole stand. Reports of a similar kid stealing *Der Viener Schlinger* and shooting another concession worker were probably circulating the security communication systems. He was sure they had connected it with him. "Wait!" Will screamed out as he realized these officers had the wrong idea. "I need you to take me to your head of security."

The officer probably thought Will was a vandalizing troublemaker who simply wanted to torment others for some sick satisfaction. Will had done what he felt he had to, but that didn't mean others would understand it yet.

"What, you've got some other way to cause trouble? I'm not going to waste my boss's time on some punk kid. I'll let the police downtown deal with you," replied the police officer.

"You're going to have to deal with a much higher level of security if you don't," Will stated curtly, letting his legs fall loose so the officer now would be forced to take more time by dragging him out of the stadium.

"Are you threatening me?" The officer yanked Will upward and shook him.

"Just take one second to radio your head of security and tell him you've got a kid who needs to see Agent Tenepior. That'll prove what I'm saying."

"I'm not falling for that. Milt Tenopir was a former Husker assistant coach, not some agent. Don't you think you've tried to get away with enough today already? Heck that concession stand is going to be shut down for the rest of the game. Don't you dare try to make stuff up around me."

Will knew he had to get himself out of this. He had to get in touch with Tenepior and let him know others would be poisoned. It occurred to him that Tenepior would most likely figure out the food was contaminated with cyanide from the powdery antidote scattered about, but only if he had time to test it to find out what the substance was.

Someone had to find out before he was removed from the stadium or the consequences would be devastating. This guard almost had him to the gate. No longer was it important to keep all this secret. If he left before these people could get help, all the secrets in the world wouldn't regain them their lives.

"Tenepior!" he shouted. The secrecy of one's identity is the first line of defense for a CovOps agent, but Will couldn't see any other way out of this situation. If another terrorist there heard his screams, Agent Tenepior's life would most likely be in danger in the near future, but his only hope was for an undercover operative to overhear and rescue him first.

A hard jerk of his arm by the officer transformed his next plea into a shriek of pain. A spasm shot up his arm as the tug cracked his elbow against the man's utility belt. A blurp from the radio at his waist squawked but the sound was muffled by Will's bawl.

Reacting in spite of the pain, Will slapped at the holstered radio with his other hand. Pinching the protruding square call button with his thumb, he shouted, "Tenepior. Gate 6!"

The clap of a hand across Will's ears made him lose his grip. "Kid, I am going to enjoy watching them lock those meddling hands of yours behind iron bars," the officer claimed, aggravated spittle scattering his foreboding words in a shower over Will's collapsed body.

Suddenly a maintenance worker charged through the standing collection of spectators. Holding a mop which he quickly threw to the ground, he grabbed the officer's arm. The officer swung his body to face the interrupting individual, hauling a slumping Will around with him.

"This is official police bus…"

But before he could even finish his claim, a shiny CIA badge had been pulled from the maintenance worker's inside coverall pocket and shoved in front of the officer's nose.

"I'll be taking over here."

12:35 P.M.

Will was immediately escorted outside and down the steps to street level. At the undercover agent's insistence, the police officer spun Will around and removed the handcuffs. The agent then led Will by his shoulder through a set of doors at the bottom center of West Stadium. Walking past glass-covered memorabilia displays that lined the walls, they entered a wide set of elevators off to the side. Once on, they didn't get off until they reached the highest level of the stadium. Moving to where the agent pointed, Will approached a line of ornately decorated dark wooden doors.

The center luxury skybox, owned by the state's largest bank, had been secured by the CIA for this operation. Having to put his weight into it, Will heaved open the heavy door. The expanse of windows now in front of him momentarily captured his attention. Overshadowing the entire football field below, the panoramic view made Will feel like he was floating in a glass bubble above the turf. The football players could have easily been a mix of X's and O's on a marker board for Will to diagram blocking schemes and draw arrows for each offensive option.

Will's eyes fluttered between the end zones as he scanned the crowd. He could feel the fans' excited energy radiating through the glass windows. Ninety one thousand was an insanely scary number he had never fully registered. Any number of these fans could already be poisoned. Breaking his astonishment for the first time, Will stammered, "Poi-poison."

"Yes. We've got a team of agents working on that right now." The familiar voice had come from Will's right. As he turned his attention in that direction, he found Agent Tenepior eyeing him, the cap of a pen held to the corner of his bottom lip. There was no joy visible behind those eyes. Where Will was hoping to find relief, the hardened look of determination in Tenepior's gaze remained steadfast.

Despite the dispirited reunion, Will was filled with relief, a relief reinforced by the removal of the coveralled maintenance worker's grip from Will's shoulder. His escort stepped leftward behind the countertop where he began unzipping his dirtied white uniform, unveiling a CIA crested black flak jacket beneath.

"Where did the poison come from?" questioned Agent Tenepior.

"The same guy who's been after me this whole time. I saw him kill some mice with it. Calls himself Azad." Will heard busy fingers typing on keyboards and knew the agents posted at computers around the room had instantly begun searching for information on the terrorist.

Turning over his shoulder to a row of Technical Security Officers, Agent Tenepior asked, "Was Azad in attendance for Umar Ghazi's hanging?"

"No, Sir. There's no record of anyone by that name present at the execution," one TSO replied.

Unsurprised by the revelation, Will continued. "Azad kidnapped me from my hotel room at the Cornhusker."

"How can that be? You never made it to your room." With one hand raised halfway into the air, an agent with dark black hair spoke from a seat against the partition wall without being called on. Though indoors, he wore silver-tinted aviator sunglasses. The gel-hardened ends of his jet-black hair cascaded over the frames. Smugness weighed upon the agent's shoulders as he leaned far backward in his cushioned chair, one lady-like leg suavely draped over the other in front of him. Gleaming white teeth sparkled from the corner of his mouth when he spoke. If he'd had a toothpick dangling there, he could have passed for a character out of some Clint Eastwood movie. There was conceit within this man's obvious urge to portray the special agent image. With one look, Will instantly felt a dislike for the man.

"What do you mean? Azad was already hiding inside my room when I got there," Will answered.

The black-haired agent replied, "We had you under surveillance when you checked in. The concierge was one of ours. But your room was never entered; the key card was never swiped." Then he rephrased his original statement into a question, "So, where exactly did you go after checking in?"

"What's with the twenty questions? And who is this guy?" asked Will turning back to Agent Tenepior.

"Will, this is Agent Rissler. We have been collaborating with Nebraska's

CIA offices to increase the number of operatives assigned to this project, especially ones familiar with the stadium and campus area. Agent Rissler's in command of all Lincoln operations, and I might add, the youngest to ever reach that status. One doesn't accomplish that without earning due respect. Therefore, his expertise and perspective is highly valuable."

"Then why doesn't he realize it's more important to figure out how to get the people in this stadium help?" questioned Will.

"We're aware of the poison; the concession stand manager was clear about that. We're just trying to piece things together," Mr. Tenepior explained.

Will's scrutiny poured across the computer monitors and other agents lining the exterior gray walls of the two-tiered room. Above them, framed pictures of Husker legends offset the clutter of equipment. Husker N insignias labeled the backs of a row of bar stools. The suite was stylish, but not extravagant. Its view made the room. Spending a couple of million dollars each year to own such a spot to seat your guests was obviously not as much about lapping up the luxury as it was about having the rights to the very best seats in all of college football. But with all the leather chairs now surrounding him, Will decided the skybox was beginning to feel more like a courtroom.

"All I know is that Azad was in the room waiting when I entered. The next thing I know, I'm waking up inside some warehouse near the Haymarket tied to Stacey."

"You located Miss Chloupek?" A hint of surprise leaked from Agent Tenepior's question.

"What, you haven't heard from her yet?" Will suddenly tensed.

"No. Where is she?"

"She was supposed to call you. She hasn't done that?" Will's voice rose as he spoke.

"There's been no word from her."

"We've got to find her. Get your men to search the campus. She was going to find a phone and call. Something must have happened!"

"We've got agents posted all around the stadium. Einstein's in charge of that crew. If she's there, he'll find her." Agent Tenepior spoke as he always did when his mind was convinced, with a finality that left little room for one to object.

Will assumed Agent Tenepior was correct because his assumptions had a way of becoming fact. As Will considered this, he stepped past Agent Rissler's seat and down the steps to the wide window front. The glass panel spanned the entire width of the room and reached almost fifteen feet to the ceiling. Up close, its clear face was larger than his eye could consume. The view spanned the expanse of Tom Osborne Field from the corner section of standing students in South Stadium to the decorative half-football edifice at the top of HuskerVision in North Stadium. When he looked directly down, he saw, just below each layer of press boxes, a foot-wide white net secured by iron to catch anything dropped through open windows.

"Are you sure Miss Chloupek isn't still being held by Azad?" asked Agent Rissler.

Will immediately turned to Mr. Tenepior and jerked his thumb in Agent Rissler's direction. "Are you sure this guy hasn't eaten a few of those Runzas?"

For once, Agent Tenepior's reply was not instantaneous. It was obvious he was selecting the right words before continuing. "Will, with what's happened today, some of our agents have become skeptical. Some things just don't seem to add up."

"Like what?"

"Like how you never ended up in the hotel room we had reserved for you," said Agent Tenepior.

One of the Technical Security Officers sitting in front of a computer stated, "It is possible this Azad hacked into the hotel's network and changed his room and electronic key card information. He may have also altered the security video footage. We know from his prior attacks on Will that he's a capable hacker."

Will smiled at the TSO, thankful that at least someone seemed to be on his side.

Nodding his head, Agent Tenepior moved on by offering another puzzling question, "How did Azad know to send the football tickets to the substation?"

"Followed us there from my house. Maybe he hacked the navigation system in your new 370Z sports car," Will curtly replied as if the answers were easily accessible.

"Why Memorial Stadium in Lincoln, Nebraska?"

"You and I both figured that must have something to do with me," Will replied. He said it quietly with his eyes on the floor as if he was ashamed to admit it.

Jumping all over Will's answer, Agent Rissler cut right in, "Probably the most accurate answer so far!" Then pushed with the hardest question to answer, "If you actually rescued Miss Chloupek, then where is she?"

That stumped Will, too.

"I believe the reason you don't have an answer," Rissler boasted, "is there's more going on here than what you've been willing to share. Azad's got Stacey and threatened to kill her unless you attack the stadium for him. He told you not to say anything, correct? You're helping this guy, aren't you!"

"That's insane!" Will shouted. He was completely amazed by the accusation. "Stacey's out there! We got away and I've been trying to stop the people in this stadium from getting sick!"

"Stop them or actually poison them?" questioned the agent.

"This guy's nuts, Mark." It was the first time he'd ever bypassed the normal respect of using a title, reminding Agent Tenepior they were not only colleagues, but friends. "Here I've single-handedly caught two terrorists and stopped a whole stand from serving any poisoned food while you've just sat here waiting for something to happen."

Agent Rissler shot out of his chair, rage obvious in his snarling teeth. "How in the world do you think you were stopping people from eating cyanide when you were the one who poisoned the food in the first place?"

That stopped Will dead in his tracks. What Rissler was insinuating simply wasn't possible. He had been stopping the poison, not spreading it. "I threw Hydroxocobalamin on that food to counter the cyanide!" he implored.

"No, what you tossed was cyanide, and we have more than twenty witnesses including a cop who say you did it on purpose."

Adamantly, Will screamed out, "That's not right! I know for a fact that Hydroxocobalamin cures cyanide. I had a bag full of it."

"You wouldn't just eat Hydroxocobalamin," Agent Rissler explained. "The liquid form gets infused through an IV."

"It cured the mice," Will shot back.

"Really? What color was this antidote?" questioned Agent Rissler.

"White," answered Will.

Rissler slowly condemned Will once and for all, punctuating each separate word with scorn. "Hydroxocobalamin is red."

Will looked at Agent Tenepior who sat there stone-faced, no contradictions to this claim on his lips.

How was this possible? He saw the mice get better in the video. The antidote was right beside the cage. He couldn't have been carrying the cyanide.

Will slumped down in a chair, completely dazed and confused. It knocked the breath clean out of him. His points had been wiped from the scoreboard. And now he was being flagged for a personal foul. If what they said was true, then everything he had done was a lie. How could he now trust his own thoughts? Was he the solution or the problem? Wracked with confusion, he didn't care at this moment that falling to the seat must have looked like an act of admission.

Agent Rissler pounced. "What else is Azad forcing you to do?" he accused.

"I haven't done anything for him. His men were the ones spreading cyanide on the Runzas."

"His men? Come on Agent Tenepior, this is completely out-of-hand," claimed Agent Rissler.

Will decided there must be something more going on here that he was unaware of, but tried to explain himself anyway. "There were two more of them. They were disguised as Runza workers. They smuggled the cyanide into the stadium when they stocked their sales stand. I stopped them both—one on a motorcycle in the Haymarket and the other disguised as an usher here in the stadium."

"That's absolutely preposterous!" shouted Agent Rissler who was glaring at Mr. Tenepior.

"Ask your security crew," Will implored. "The guy I shot with a pepper shaker is being detained by one of your agents underneath the stands."

Finally Mr. Tenepior chimed in. "Will, we know all about him. The guy you knocked out happened to be an undercover CIA operative from my own task force. He was assigned to surveillance posts in multiple stadium locations. That's why he was in two different disguises. One of Agent Rissler's men found his badge while doing a body search and called it in to us. He reported that you had taken off by the time he found it."

"And you claim he was a terrorist!" spat Agent Rissler.

Agent Tenepior ignored the comment and continued, "The motorcyclist was one of ours as well. Einstein was trying to track your cell phone and sent the agent to check out a possible lead on your whereabouts. At least now we can piece together what happened to him. Unfortunately, he's in surgery with multiple injuries and we've been unable to communicate with him."

"But you already knew this, didn't you!" Agent Rissler screamed. "You attacked them to carry out your plan!"

Will felt like he'd been hit by a linebacker. It was almost too much to take in. This couldn't be happening. Was it simple chance those two agents appeared in Azad's video? Will knew the footage was stolen from stadium surveillance video. Did Azad simply show real scenes of the men working undercover and manipulate Will into believing they were stocking the poison?

"Why are you attacking our own men? What did they catch you doing?" challenged Agent Rissler.

"Nothing!" cried Will. Too confused to understand it all, he shot back with the only truth he knew, "You just find Azad. He's the one you want—not me."

"If you're helping him, that makes you guilty, too!" charged Agent Rissler.

Tenepior shot Agent Rissler a hard glance.

Agent Rissler didn't back off. "Your make-believe story is the craziest fantasy I've ever heard. You've forcibly attacked two government agents, smuggled a deadly toxin into a public place, intentionally tried using it to poison people, and withheld evidence from an investigation. How can you claim you did nothing? Do I need to continue poking holes through your story or will you save us time and simply admit to the wrongdoing?"

Why did they think he had messed this all up? He had always tried his best to do the right thing. He wouldn't hurt anyone without a good reason to do so. "I didn't mean to do anything wrong!"

"You've got to be kidding me! Your actions are evidence. Admit it and share what you know before it's too late! Is Stacey how he's controlling you? Where is she being held? What else is he forcing you to do?" shouted Agent Rissler.

"That's enough!" commanded Tenepior. He had risen and walked to the kitchenette countertop. His shuffle was slow and he stared at the ground as he moved. Leaning both forearms across the counter, he shook his head as he began to speak. "What you're claiming just isn't Will. The only rational thing to believe at this point is that he's been tricked into all this. He didn't do any of it on purpose. I don't believe he'd be a willing participant unless he thought he was doing the right thing. And even if Stacey was being used as blackmail, I think Will would choose to save the larger number of lives. He's risked his own to do so before."

Just as Mr. Tenepior finished his defense of Will, a pounding on the door broke the tension. Another agent stepped through, his face white with worry. "Agent Starks who was working Gate 24 was just found dead in one of the service entrances."

The room quaked as Mr. Tenepior's balled hand struck the counter.

Will figured the dead agent must be the one who called him "Little Duckling" and chased after Azad.

The agent at the door continued, "Agent Starks was gripping this." In his hands he held up a red piece of frayed cloth.

Agent Rissler strode over to the agent and reached out to examine the fabric. Rolling it methodically between his fingers and taking a thorough examination of it, he pinched a corner letting the rest hang loose. Then he took a long look at Will. Making a great show of things, he held it out toward Will's shoulder. The torn cloth was an exact match of his missing shirt sleeve.

1:05 P.M.

"Agent Starks? Found dead? How?" asked Agent Tenepior.

"Head injury," stated the agent at the door.

Tenepior looked at Will for a long moment and then changed his gaze to Agent Rissler.

Will could only guess what he was thinking.

"I need to check on this myself," stated Agent Tenepior as he grabbed for the door. His face was all scrunched up and his eyes darted all around the room.

For the first time since meeting Agent Tenepior, Will thought he looked frazzled.

"Nobody leaves this skybox," Tenepior ordered and shut the wooden door behind him.

Will was left alone with a room full of agents, but without an ally. He felt like Tenepior, the only one who had known and had believed in Will from the start, had just fed him to the wolves. He guessed by Agent Tenepior's hasty departure that his resolve in Will's innocence was wavering so he had to directly inspect the body to rule out other possibilities. Never gambling with his conclusions, the man was loyal to his men, but it was evident that all bets were being placed on the "Don't Pass Line."

Will couldn't take his eyes off the closed door. Agent Rissler, who had exerted himself against Will from the start, stood from his chair and ordered two of the agents to seize Will. The agents roughly grabbed Will's arms and pulled them behind his back. Rissler waited until Will was held firmly and then started right back in with his accusations. "What'd you do to Agent Starks, you little creep?"

"I didn't do anything to him. Last time I saw him, he was running after the terrorist."

"Then why was Agent Starks holding your torn shirt sleeve?"

"The terrorist ripped it. I'd forgotten all about it until now."

"The terrorist ripped it? Or did Agent Starks catch you doing something before you spread the cyanide? Speak the truth!"

"I haven't lied! If you're such a hot shot why can't you figure that out?" Will challenged.

"You claim you haven't done anything wrong. Am I imagining that you brought cyanide into the stadium? Did I make up the part where you intentionally threw poison on food about to be eaten? Are you saying we somehow misheard your confession of attacking two CIA agents? How about the fact that a dead agent was found holding fabric from your clothing?" Agent Rissler attacked back.

"It may look that way, but that's not what happened."

"Those are facts!" Agent Rissler screamed.

"I'm not the problem. Why can't you see that! You've got to be the dumbest agent I've ever met. I'll never get why Tenepior trusts your judgment," said Will.

"Trusts me? I've never done something as stupid as you; you can't even deny any of this! The real question is what does Agent Tenepior see in you?" Agent Rissler then paused and gripped a chair back with both hands, lowering his voice when he spoke. "Agent Starks was one of the good guys. He was one of us. You're just some kid. Finding a lucky clue in some shoe commercial doesn't make you an operative. As I see it, all you're good at is getting blackmailed. Either this Azad has something on you or you are doing this of your own free will. That makes you a problem that needs taken care of. And my job is to neutralize liabilities."

Since none of the operatives had a set of handcuffs, Agent Rissler decided to unplug an electrical cord from the wall outlet and wrap it around Will's wrists. The cord bit into his skin. It pinched tightly with each thin wrap, a terse reminder of the tight situation he was wound up in. Agent Rissler seemed to use the anger produced from his fellow agent's murder to pull the cord tighter than necessary, constricting the blood flow to Will's hands and causing a sensation of tiny cold pins to poke his palms. The forked plug dangled from the extra length of cord. With any movement, it knocked into the back of his knee, prodding him to come up with a way out of this confinement.

Though deemed a luxury box, the skybox was now a prison. From his angle, the window caught the glaring light of the early afternoon sun, further entrapping him behind the feeling of one-way glass. Left standing in the middle of the floor, Will was unable to even glimpse through the window far enough beyond the crowd to see the game being played on the field below. He would be denied that simple pleasure. The agents around him continued with tasks of surveillance, but kept a second, suspicious eye on Will, as if waiting to counter his next play.

Unrelenting in his innocence, Will stood defiantly, not allowing his knees to shake and keeping his legs locked to show he wouldn't buckle under pressure. He didn't want Agent Rissler to know how badly he wanted one of the chairs to rest on. He knew his stance would give the appearance of being proud, a look that many would read as guilt, but the accusations against him claimed that he was an accomplice to terror activity. He knew he had done his best to be the one who saved lives.

Will wanted to cry out that they weren't being fair—that there was still a terrorist on the loose who was capable of great harm. He wanted to explain that he honestly thought he had brought an antidote into the stadium instead of the toxin. How could he have known the antidote was red? He wished he had been more thorough in his research instead of thinking he knew it all from experience. He'd have found out more about Hydroxocobalamin and other countermeasures. If he could just go back in time, he'd have recognized that one little detail and kept this mess from happening, but that just wasn't possible.

Finishing the last wrap of cord, Agent Rissler came forward and took a long look at Will. "I'd normally recommend that you wash your hands in case you've contaminated yourself with cyanide. It wouldn't be good for your health to have it soaking into your skin. But, as it is, it happens to be evidence that will prove you tried poisoning the fans at this game. It would only be fitting for you to writhe in your own poison."

"I didn't touch it, so you won't get the satisfaction!" Will spat back. "You'll wish you treated me better when Tenepior sees this. He knows I'm innocent. And I seem to be the only one trying to stop the actual criminal. This," he said, raising his bound hands as if stretching his triceps, "is stopping your best chance at catching him. I know what he looks like. And you are preventing me from trying to get this guy?"

"Agent Tenepior may have let his personal friendship with you cloud his judgment, but I see through your plan. You see, we spend every day tracking and investigating terror plots to determine who needs to be watched and how to stop their evil plotting. This is one plot I aim to make certain doesn't go any further. Agent Starks and I were Academy brothers and I owe it to him to ensure you don't cause any more harm."

"I have done nothing wrong," Will stated emphatically.

"You see all these screens? As you stand there, these Technical Security Officers are searching for any signs of your terrorist and footage of your actions."

Replaying across monitors throughout the skybox were distant rewound shots of Will shooting an agent with *Der Viener Schlinger* and pulling the bag of cyanide from his waistline before chucking its contents throughout the concession stand. Will could see how they made him look guilty. The footage shown so far wouldn't do much to prove his innocence. He thought it was unfortunate there weren't more cameras below stadium or his story might have had evidence to his truthfulness. He strained to see the faces in the crowds on the monitors. One glimpse and they'd have their man. If they weren't able to catch a shot of his attacker, then Will's story would carry little weight.

Agent Rissler said, "From what I see, your lies won't stand up to what the video shows."

"When Stacey's found, she'll give you the exact story I did," answered Will.

"Come on! You can stop with the charade. Where is Azad and where is he holding Miss Chloupek? Don't you realize he's not going to let Stacey go no matter what you help him do? Help us catch him right now so we can end all this. Tell us where he is and what else he is planning to do!"

Will wasn't entirely sure if it was the words Rissler used or the tone of his voice, but in that statement he recalled the YouTube clip of the terrorist's rancorous petitions before his hanging. That man had thought his actions were justified. His eyes had held no guilt because that's not what his twisted mind believed.

Did this make Will any different? He also thought he had done the right thing. Did believing you were doing the right thing make you the bad guy to those who disagree with your actions? He had been set up. But it was his own hands that had thrown the poison. Was he guilty if he didn't realize its harm? At least one agent definitely thought so.

Here he was, facing almost the same predicament as a terrorist who had *intentionally* attacked American people. How had he fallen so easily into this trap? It had all gone exactly the way Azad had planned. The words of his attacker flooded his mind, "…maybe then my brother will find his peace. It will give me great pleasure knowing you are feeling the pain he felt in his execution."

Had Azad intended for him to take the blame all along? Will knew he couldn't let this happen. The men in this room might not be able to locate any video evidence in his favor, but he had video of his own. "I've got proof!" he yelled out as the thought struck him. His scream clearly shocked everyone as they quickly turned his way. "In my pocket. I stole a thumb drive from the terrorist's computer that shows his plans to smuggle the cyanide into the stadium and the mice he killed completing the experiment. I swear it's the truth. Just look in my right pocket."

His interrogator pulled himself to his feet. He wasted no time getting to Will's side, digging abruptly through the side pocket of his cargo shorts. Palming the rectangular device, he gave Will a long, hard look. Pushing the thumb drive forward, he handed it to a Technical Security Officer.

"Hurry! There's still time to get these people medical help if they've been poisoned."

The thumb drive was inserted into the USB port of the networked computer.

"The clip will first show the Runza workers I encountered," Will offered.

Pressing the left mouse button, the tech agent activated the external device. Moving the cursor across the screen, he double-clicked on the one file found.

Will continued, "You'll see how he created his plan and how he saved two mice with the antidote."

The file opened.

Wide-eyed, Will tensed, leaning his body way forward, waiting for the vindication the video would bring. At the same moment the screen brightened not with a video, but with the white background of a title page as a document opened. A shudder rippled through his body as his eyes starred dumbly at the words filling the center of the screen: "How to Pull off the Perfect Act of Terrorism: An I-Search paper by Will Conlan."

The scraping sound of a chair's leg scooting backward across the floor and the gasps of almost every seated operative filled the room with a unified hiss. Seconds passed in absolute silence. Will stood dumbstruck, his fixed eyes unblinking. Gaping mouths enveloped the room with darkened, breathless voids. Slowly, these unmoving lips began to thin and stretch around moist teeth, provoked into anger and ready to bite. Each agent turned to face him, ferocious hate pulsing from reddening eyes.

The undercurrent of a hum began to rumble beneath their feet. If it weren't for the absolute silence in the skybox, it would have been undetectable. Will thought his shaking body was causing the whole room to vibrate. The technologist turned sharply to his computer and quickly clicked through a series of windowed options. The humming intensified as the large glass stadium-facing window began to shimmer. With the game's excitement on the field below, the fans seemed unfazed by the rumbling, probably assuming it was the buzz of the entire crowd's excitement.

Suddenly the thumb drive flew across the room. The TSO had yanked it from the computer like an insect plucked from someone's back. "The whole network's been breached. He infected it with a worm!"

This time it wasn't an accusation. Agent Rissler, who had verbally accosted him from the time he entered, turned to face Will, his outstretched arm surging with animosity.

Just as Agent Rissler took his first step toward him, Will looked away to his left, suddenly distracted by a screeching noise. He locked his gaze on HuskerVision's gigantic stadium speaker. He knew the 335,000 watt sound system was recently installed as part of a stadium expansion project. The state-of-the-art audio system was supposed to be the most sophisticated in college football. Will suspected instantly what this viral worm was programmed to attack and slapped his cupped hands over his ears.

A screeching sound wave blasted from the speaker, its perforated grill pulsating with its tremor. The rupture of noise was so intense that he saw fans seated below the speaker collapsing into a human debris field across the bench seats. The intensity of the air blast drowned out what Will knew must be the savage screams of the ear-clutching victims. The closest of the skyboxes burst, the great front windows shattering with the piercing wave of sound.

Shrieking with similar intensity, some agent from across the skybox screamed, "That had to be over 165 decibels! That's way beyond a person's threshold for pain!"

Will imagined that the eardrums of tens of thousands must have shattered instantly. He saw many of the toppled victims convulsing with seizures or grasping at their chests. As he watched, the center skybox's window cracked exactly at the spot he was peering through, leaving long jagged streaks of angled crevices across its expanse.

The security officer yelled, "It's not turning off!"

Just then a second high-energy-impulse noise blasted from the speaker. Though everyone bent their waists as if bracing themselves, it became evident the tempered glass of their skybox was shielding them from greater harm. Cracks elongated, scaring the protective unit with deep, irreversible dissension. Every agent's head was turned toward the stadium. Many stood defensively crouched on the balls of their feet, apparently ready to immediately act on any orders. Where most of the people in the southern half of the stadium were clearly injured, no one in the skybox was suffering enough to sink entirely to his knees.

The people just below them on the upper deck didn't look as fortunate. With each acoustic bullet, more writhing people toppled to the stands. In a chaotic frenzy, fans were throwing themselves toward exits.

The instant this second blast was over, the men in the skybox began scrambling. The techies furiously worked their keyboards as security agents charged out the door. Looking around at all the movement, Will saw one particular agent, a man whose suspicion had obviously now turned to hatred, charging directly at him.

1:17 P.M.

The guttural cry of hostility that screamed from deep within Agent Rissler intensified the piercing volume of the simultaneous acoustic blast from the speaker, almost knocking Will over. Surging forward, the operative stormed toward him. His suit coat sleeves tightened around his biceps as he lunged for Will.

Will simply reacted. It wasn't the time to weigh options or hope for a better outcome. As his dad would have put it, "When the wind's in your face, you've gotta grab for paddles." Bending his knees and gritting his teeth, Will sprang from his feet, landing on top of the partitioning half-wall that separated the room into its second tier. Leaping with all his strength over the heads of the agents below, he jumped straight toward the cracked window. Kicking out, he pulled his legs in front of him midair. His feet smacked the square of glass before exploding through. A riot of glass pebbles burst from the window pane. Ruptured, oval-shaped crystals sparkled around him as he flew outward through the open air.

Another acoustic blast slammed him sideways just as he erupted through the skybox's shattered cavity. The gust of sound was so powerful it blew his backside onto the opened top hung window pane two press boxes over. The window only managed to slow his fall as the glass shattered beneath him on impact and his body fell through. His wrists and feet banged recklessly against its rectangular metal casing as his body folded through and plummeted another ten feet before crashing into thin netting placed beneath the last set of press box windows. If it hadn't been for the foot-wide protective nets, his jump might have been deadly. He flipped his body over the edge and fell the remaining dozen feet, breaking his fall on the backs of several disoriented spectators sprawled over the club level's seats.

As he rolled off of their collapsed bodies, he wasn't sure his crash against them fully registered. They already seemed in enough pain. Will managed to pull his tied-up arms around his rear and legs until they were out in front of him. Guessing he only had another second or two before the next sound blast struck, he tried sheltering himself by summersaulting over a heavyset man who was lying on his side and rocking back and forth. Jamming his fingertips into his own ears and crouching low behind the rocking body, Will used the man's bulk as a human shield just as another concussion ripped through the air. The man knocked against his body from the force of the blast and temporarily pinned Will's body to the cement between two rows of red seats.

Will tried to jerk his legs free, but the man was not rolling off, clearly in enough pain that moving seemed a chore. Will shoved at the man's shoulder to lift some of the weight from his legs and pulled them free. The press of his hands seemed to rouse the man as he looked straight at Will for the first time, his pained eyes pleading through tears.

"I'll help you, but you've got to untie this cord first." Will held up his wrists as he spoke.

The man simply stared back, hands still clamped at the sides of his head, a trickle of blood draining between his fingers. Will realized the man could not hear a word he had said. Gesturing with his wrists turned upward, he flung his head in the direction of the closest exit at the top of the stairs. The man must have understood as he reached out with a single hand and pulled at one end of the cord secured about Will's wrists. His other hand remained at his ear.

His downward yank loosened a strand enough that Will was able to pull his wrists apart, slackening the cord. It allowed him to use one hand to assist the man with unlooping the next strand. Tugging back as hard as he could, Will was able to wrench his hands free. The morning's knot had provided good practice, and yet that rope had been so much easier to untangle. Stacey had incredibly detangled that rope with her hands behind her back. Or was Stacey just that much better at knots? Lightning-quick guesses flooded suspicion through his thoughts. Was it possible he was meant to escape all along? The terrorist must have predicted Will would snatch the bag of cyanide and swipe the thumb drive.

He glanced at the speaker above HuskerVision's jumbo screen. He eyed the giant twenty-five foot illuminated red "N" and knew the sixth sound blast would be only seconds away. Darting his head around as he looked for something to cover his ears, he grabbed a light jacket someone had dropped. Will wrapped it around his head and tied it at the back as a makeshift bandana before spotting a discarded hot dog beneath a seat. Ripping two chunks and jabbing them hard into each ear, he slid the jacket down to cover them before turning back to the man.

Unable to hear anything himself now, he still believed the next sound wave might possibly cause some damage. It occurred to him then that he had seen the terrorist wearing orange earplugs. If that was his precaution, then maybe Will didn't have to worry as much, but to be extra cautious, he waved his hands downward signaling the man to drop once again. This time he didn't use him as a shield, but rather than thinking just of himself, he huddled into a ball with him, trying to protect them both.

Feeling the force of the air blast hit his body without fully hearing the shrill noise made Will realize that the true destructive power came from the overpressurized air flow smacking into people. If it had been much stronger or had people been any closer, Will thought the force could possibly be intense enough to rupture lung tissue and send fatal air bubbles through a person's arteries to their heart and brain. He hoped the sixteen high-directional sound beam speakers were already maxed out, but he didn't want to stick around to find out.

Jumping to his feet, Will suddenly noticed the man had begun to clutch his chest, balling up his replica jersey between fingers so that two white numbers twisted into one. Panicked at what the last blast had done to him, Will leaned backward into him, pulling a heavy arm over his shoulder and around his chest in an effort to half piggyback, half drag the man up the steps to the exit.

As Will made his way up, people were rushing past them, trying to save themselves. He realized that with the acoustic attack, the normal hospitable confines of Memorial Stadium had transformed people into their weaker, self-preserving selves. The pandemonium was maddening. People were running about and screaming in such confusion that no organized evacuation maneuver would have been possible. And though each person's terror was making it more difficult for the few able-bodied security personnel still standing to marshal an effort, he realized it was creating the exact cover he needed.

As he clamored up the steps to the top of the club level, the man's left leg dragged and limply thumped against each cemented edge. What weight he wasn't placing on his right was being hefted by Will's back and broad shoulders, now fully draped by the man's heavy arm and chest. New beads of sweat permeated Will's forehead with each step he struggled to crest.

The man's other hand was still gripped at his chest. His nails dug wide holes through the perforation of his jersey as he sipped at short breaths.

Without warning, the weight lessened. Instead of being hunched over under the bulk as he had been, Will was suddenly able to stand erect. If it had not been for the arm still wrapped around his shoulder, he'd have thought the man had fallen to the stairs. Then he noticed a new shoulder had appeared next to his. Some man had come to his aid by wrapping his arm around the injured man's waist.

Will didn't hesitate. With a second person helping, he made a run for it. Security was surely coming for him and this man had definitely slowed his escape. But Will wasn't trying to make a getaway. He had guessed the man's pain. It wasn't Will's own life he had run off to save.

Will knew most sporting venues housed defibrillators. A stadium would have several. Charging into a first aid station just down the carpeted hallway, he spotted one within seconds. Hanging on a wall, its fluorescent green casing made it easy to spot. He pressed his thumb to the power button as he ran back. He found both men crashed to the floor of the concourse.

Using the scissors he found inside the plastic box, he cut the Rex Burkhead jersey at the man's chest between the "twos," trying not to think about his destruction of such an awesome shirt. Slapping the electrode pads to the man's chest he fired the shock button. After a quick scream of pain, the tension immediately left the man. His body noticeably relaxed, shoulders easing to the ground.

A Red Cross worker who had been assisting some wheelchaired spectators came running. The man lifted his hand and grabbed Will's forearm. A look of appreciation passed between the two that made Will feel ashamed. Though the man would probably never know it, Will was the reason for his pain, *not* his healing.

Will couldn't stick around, especially now that his new friend seemed to be doing better. Agent Rissler had most likely seen him drop to the club seats and probably was already down at this level searching for him.

Looking around, he spotted TVs in corners and even a wooden barbeque stand constructed in the large hallway. Injured people leaned against circular, bar-height tables in the large standing area that looked out over Pinnacle Bank's Husker basketball arena. There wasn't much of a place to hide. He needed a way out, and he decided that dissolving into the larger crowds of the lower stadium was his best bet.

Just as he thought it, he caught a glimpse of Agent Rissler charging out of the elevators toward him. He was close enough for Will to read his lips as he screamed, "Get that boy!"

Enclosed by walls on three sides, Will knew he would quickly be trapped. He glanced in every direction and then to the stadium bleachers. It had been the way he had just come, but it was his only option out. Its dangers seemed a better option than facing Rissler.

Rushing back down the steps to the outdoor seating, he frantically searched for a way down. Jumping three steps at a time, he ran to the red railing that marked the edge of the balcony. Looking over, he saw that the benches were empty of spectators. There would be no nets or people this time to help break his fall, and he was not anxious to jump from this balcony even though the fall would be about a third of the distance as his last. It had hurt enough the last time.

Agent Rissler came running out the most northern door to the club seats. His eyes locked onto Will. He continued charging, obviously trying to pin him into the corner where a jump would be his only escape. Will had already ruled that out.

While it would bring him closer to Rissler, he ran back up the steps and then directly away from this pursuer to the southernmost part of the elevated stand. In the corner stood a twenty-foot-wide, square, cement pillar. The cornerstones of the stadium rose like giant pyramids anchoring the four bleacher sections. The stone structure was topped with tiered beige blocks. During games an usher would be positioned in these corners so no one would try climbing over the railing to the step pyramid at the support's top. That's exactly what Will had in mind.

With great strides he leaped up five tiered steps to the top. Hurrying, he launched himself over to its side and away from Rissler's sight. He could see the pillar's square backside was lined with decorative lips that gave it a crown molding look. Stepping to the front edge and looking down over one of the cornered HuskerVision boards, Will saw his way down. He wasn't going to jump, but he wanted Rissler to think he had so he wouldn't be followed.

Using the metal braces that secured the video board to the cement front of the pillar as handholds, he quickly lowered himself down to the lip rimming the bottom of the giant block and jumped to the stairs from there. Running to his left across the south stands, he looked back over his shoulder. Rissler was peering over at him from the pillar's top. Sure he had been seen, Will dove through the first exit ramp he came to.

About ten feet down, Will stopped. He was sure there'd be agents waiting for him at the ramp's bottom. He couldn't go down there. If that's where Agent Rissler thought he was headed, his best option would be to disappear to the opposite side of the stadium. Knowing Rissler had seen him with the jacket wrapped around his head, he untied it and allowed it to drop to the concrete. Because of the next move he knew he had to make, its removal was a risk.

He waited, catching his breath until he thought Rissler had most likely left the stands and paused for the next sound blast. By timing his next move just as the sound blast hit, he might catch any onlookers with their heads down. When the blast came, he retraced his steps back out to the stadium seats in a sprint.

Even though this plan would take him closer to the speaker's blast and nearer potential physical harm, he had to get away and keep the authorities guessing. It would be illogical to think he'd run toward the giant speaker. And that made it his best chance of escape. If he could make it out and away from the stadium, he might even get the chance to find the answers he needed.

As he ran across the turf, he promised himself that he'd find the man who had set all this in motion. Even if it took his dying breath, he would prove his innocence. The truth had to be found and his name had to be cleared. The world had to know he wasn't behind all this.

But until then, he intended to stay the bad guy. There was no other way, really, for what he knew it would take to redeem himself. The terrorist would not get the better of him again. Will would make him pay.

He could no longer be anyone's puppet.

His moves would return to being his.

If his good intentions made him easy to manipulate, then Will would simply have to act differently. He had been so focused on stopping the poison, he had missed his chance to take down his real opponent. Maybe the key to catching this guy was putting people at risk instead of trying to save them. This seemed unreasonable, but nothing else had worked his way, so maybe he would try the opposite. Since everyone in the country was going to believe he was evil, he figured the terrorist should too. Pulling from his father's wise words, it only made sense that if this guy wanted to plant corn, then he was going to get corn. It was time, he decided, to make his attacker fear his retaliation. You brought this fight to me, Will thought, so now it's my turn to bring it to you.

TEENAGER IMPLICATED IN AUDIO ASSAULT

By Arnold Barry
OMAHA TIMES CORRESPONDENT

LINCOLN, Neb. — The tragedy in Lincoln during Saturday's Nebraska Huskers and Northwestern Wildcats football game has now been labeled an act of terrorism. The repeated sound bursts from the stadium's south speaker cluster were not caused by computer malfunction as first reported, but rather from a cyber attack mounted by Will Conlan, a fifteen-year-old boy.

Donovan Rissler, a regional CIA Counterterrorism Analyst, confirmed Conlan used a thumb drive to implant a carefully constructed viral weapon into the stadium's network. Details on how he gained access to the computer systems are still unknown.

Once uploaded, the worm disguised its presence to move throughout the network unnoticed until it disrupted the pitch and volume of HuskerVision's speaker system. Each high-energy-impulse noise, sometimes referred to as acoustic bullets by the military, shot multiple air blasts through the stadium, injuring mostly those nearest the speakers. Similar air blasts have accounted for deaths among soldiers of war who were near explosions but suffered no external injuries.

Conlan's involvement was uncovered, Rissler said, as witnesses came forward claiming a teenager screaming "People are going to die!" attacked two food service vendors, and vandalized a concession stand. Upon investigation, it was determined he tossed a bag of crystalized cyanide into the stand. This toxin, if ingested, could potentially be fatal.

Benedict Snodgrass, Conlan's AP English instructor at Mount Prospect High School near Chicago, described him as a troubled youth who fantasized about becoming a terrorist. "He even copied his work from presidential counterterrorism speeches," he told reporters. For a recent assignment, Conlan wrote a report detailing plans to contaminate mobile food stands at public gatherings. Witnesses near the concession stand claimed the troubled teen was laughing after he released the cyanide.

Of the sixteen lives lost in the attack, none were caused by cyanide poisoning. Cardiac arrest and strokes accounted for nine fatalities while seven were victims of falling or being trampled to death. Over 20,000 people are currently receiving medical attention for ruptured ear drums and hearing loss.

Conlan managed to elude security officials and escape the stadium unapprehended. Any persons with information on his whereabouts should contact their local law enforcement agency. The FBI has added the teen to their list of ten most wanted. This marks the first time since Timothy McVeigh that a homegrown terrorist has become America's number one criminal.

October 25, Somewhere on U.S. Highway 6

3:00 P.M.

The wind whipped through his hair, cooling him from the afternoon's sun. Stowed away between bales on the back of a hay truck, Will lay on his back, low and unseen. The speed at which he traveled down the highway comforted him. For the time being, the more miles he put between him and Agent Rissler, the better.

Hot rays sweltered down from clear skies above. A red hue had begun to form on his face and arms. He welcomed the burn's sting, a beginning penance well deserved for the suffering he'd inflicted on so many innocent lives.

He had somehow managed to make it to this point relatively unharmed. Granted he had become a fugitive of the law, but he had managed to make it out of the stadium without any hearing loss or internal injury.

In his flight across the football field, he had ducked through the tunnel leading back to the locker rooms in the Tom and Nancy Osborne Athletic Complex underneath North Stadium. He had hidden himself away in a laundry cart used by the players to dump their sweaty, soiled uniforms. About nearly suffocating himself beneath the sweaty piles of jerseys, he had become worried the athletic department had its own laundry facilities within the complex and dug himself out to find another spot to hide.

He found it in a side compartment of a fire truck that had been called to the scene. Quietly opening a rear hatch large enough for him to easily squeeze into, he had folded his body around the generator and Jaws of Life it stored. It hadn't been comfortable, but it had been secure; he couldn't at the time think of a reason why anyone would open this compartment at the stadium. Luckily, no one had.

He pulled a stem of hay that caught in the frayed edges of his torn shirt sleeve. Almost lost in the swirling breeze, it clung hard to its last hope against the fury of the imposing wind. Splintered at one end, its role in keeping the bale whole seemed to be ripped apart. Now unattached, it was unlikely it would ever be reclaimed.

Instead of letting the stem go with the next gust, Will stuck it upright between his teeth, letting the wind whip at it, but keeping it pinned in his firm hold. For a moment, it felt good to cling to something so tangible and real. Knowing he had been so easily fooled and taken advantage of pulled apart his pride. The terrorists' intent to poison people had been all too easy to believe after seeing the mice eat the powder and die. Convinced by the footage he'd viewed, it had been reasonable to think the Runza employees had indeed smuggled the toxin into the stadium. How was he to know the young men had been secretly filmed and had no actual part? After all, the surveillance video his terrorist obviously had hacked into clearly showed these two stocking shelves with bags of some sort of spices.

And in a genius play, he had been duped into smuggling in the deadly toxin. The terrorist hadn't risked doing it himself. It pained Will to realize this may have been a larger objective than actually poisoning the crowd. It succeeded in framing Will for bioterrorism and implicated him in the same crime for which the terrorist's friend had been hung. Will wondered if his own subsequent terrorism trial and execution, had he been caught, was actually the terrorist's main priority. He recalled the precision of words his attacker had used: "It is all to be your death penalty."

But how had the terrorist predicted Will would also unleash the worm into the stadium's electronic network? Had it been as simple as guessing he would indeed swipe the thumb drive as proof? He should have seen through it all. Hadn't the terrorist bragged about his programming and hacking capabilities? Didn't he even admit he had tricks up his sleeves?

The clues had been right there. His failure to connect the dots frustrated him as much as anything. Pulling the stem from his mouth, he rolled it between his fingers. The dried straw felt hollow and he lifted it to his eye to peer through. A tiny blue dot of sky appeared far through the end. It occurred to him that this was exactly how he'd been seeing things. His narrowed focus had been like tunnel vision where he couldn't see the full picture.

Lying there looking through the hollowed stem, he continued to think about what he wasn't seeing. For one thing he had missed the action between his two favorite teams or what game there had been before it was suspended.

His two favorite teams.

Sticking the straw back into his mouth, he chewed on that thought for a while. Was it possible Memorial Stadium wasn't a specific target? Could this whole plot have been centered on himself?

It wouldn't be hard to guess that a Chicago boy would be a Northwestern fan. But it would have been difficult for the terrorist to know he also rooted for the Huskers. Nothing in this puzzle could be a coincidence. They rarely were in these circumstances. Each clue, if a shape could be seen, interlocked the piece into a pattern. And yet, to Will, the puzzle's center piece still seemed shapeless, unable to fit. How had Azad known to send these specific tickets to the CIA substation? Only a few select people knew of his affiliation with the agency.

A puppet master knows what strings to pull. And Will knew his strings had been all too easy to tug. He was sure very few people on Earth would not only have the resources at their fingertips to attach those strings, but also possess the soft touch to jerk and waggle his actions with such guile and deftness.

Agent Tenepior had suspected foul play. Maybe it was true; Agent Tenepior's hunches were never far off.

The real perpetrator in this crime seemed to know Will's own thinking. And he was cunning enough to use it against him. It was as if the terrorist understood Will inside and out.

Flinging the straw stem away into the wind, Will suddenly realized he had an idea who may have been responsible. If right, he would make the disloyal man pay for his betrayal. He had to find the truth to make it all right. It was his only true path to redemption.

Acknowledgments

A special thanks to Nancy Lazer for up-close access to my favorite setting of all time and for Joseph Krueger's creativity with the art inserts and cover design. I am grateful for the guidance Jeff Weeks provided to make technical aspects of the story reasonable. Thanks to Stu Burns and David Waller for the thoughtful editorial insights and suggestions.

CPSIA information can be obtained at www.ICGtesting.com
Printed in the USA
LVOW07s1830081215

465958LV00004B/832/P

9 781491 773697